Almost as soon as the bullet hit him, Tit Smith knew that someone had made a mistake. In all his sixteen years in Cornwall, Vermont, no one cared a hoot about "Millie's boy"—not enough to blow him open. But to kill Millie? Yes, there were reason to kill a woman like his mother.

Mysteries haunted Tit: Who killed his ma? Who was his pa? And who, really, was he? Gus Tobin, the raw-handed sheriff who cut the lead out of his belly, kept a shut mouth. So did the mule-driving woman doctor, Fern Bodeen. She patched up Tit's body right, and tried even harder to mend his spirit. But neither Fern nor her pretty niece Amy Hallow, could solve the mystery of Tit Smith.

So he headed North, back to where his life had begun, into an 1898 Adirondack wilderness. There, locked in the silent cold and deep snow of Ironville, were the answers to Tit Smith's life. . . .

Here is an exciting, action-packed novel which combines adventure, romance and suspense.

MILLIE'S BOY

Robert Newton Peck

MILLIE'S BOY

Alfred A. Knopf

New York

cop. 2

1-74 BT 495

Library of Congress Cataloging in Publication Data

Peck, Robert Newton.   Millie's Boy

Summary: A boy searches for his real father and encounters many adventures along the way. I. Title. PZ7.P339Mi [Fic] ISBN 0-394-82699-X   ISBN 0-394-92699-4 (lib. bdg.)

to Sheriff Clyde Peck
of Bennington County, Vermont—
who was one good lawman.

MILLIE'S BOY

1

When the gun went off in the dark of that tiny room, all I saw was a big orange blast of powder.

I didn't see the gun, or who triggered it. For a few seconds, I thought I heard voices, and boots scraping against the floor and going down the back stairs like they was in a big hurry. But my ears were ringing, so I couldn't of heard too much.

The room was black, and I didn't make out a thing. And all I could sense was the sulphur stink of spent gunpowder, a real yellow smell. It was a second or two before I took notice of the main problem, the fact that I'd been hit to the floor. And that I had one hell of a hurting gut.

"Tit," I said to myself, "you been shot."

That was about when the numb feeling of getting knocked silly began to leave go of me, and the hot pain in my belly took over. It wasn't so

1

bad at first when I just lied still. But when I started to crawl, I thought my insides were on fire. My whole body doubled up in a cramp and froze there, like I was afraid to move. When I curled up, my head slid down across the wood of the floor toward where my belly had been, and it slid real good. Too good. On account of which, I was skidding around in the warm slime of my own blood.

I moved again. It almost made me scream, but that would of made little sense. Whoever it was with the gun might yet be around, and would come back to finish me off. I wondered who it was. As far as I knew, I didn't have an enemy in the world. Maybe there was a few of the boys at school who hadn't taken to me, like Whit Whitcomb and Bud Wayne—but I didn't think they hated me enough to kill me. Beat me up, maybe; or take off my trousers and throw 'em in the horse trough. But not shoot me up on a Saturday night and leave me for dead. It had to be Millie he was after.

"Millie," I said. It was the first thing I could say out loud, and it even hurt to talk. I sure was hoping she'd hear me, or that somebody would.

"Millie. Millie, I'm hit and bleeding. You in bed?"

My eyes were growing used to the dark and I could see a bit. Raising my head up off the sticky floor, I started to wonder about just where I was. When I come home, I come up the front stairs and into the kitchen. But I must of pitched forward through the curtain and into Millie's room. Moving my leg, my foot kicked a wall. My eyes squinted through the blackness and I could make out a ball, one of the brass balls on the four corners of Millie's four-poster. The bed was all messed up, as it always was; but my mother wasn't in it. She usually was, alongside a man or a bottle.

But there was a bottle. Crawling forward, I brushed my face against its cork. The bottle was on its side and empty, lying at the edge of the white, egg-shaped rug beside the bed.

That little soft white rug was one of my mother's special comforts. Millie hated to get out of bed for much of anything; but even less if it meant touching her toes to a cold floor.

"Millie," I called in a half whisper.

Pulling myself up on the bed, the smell (that I had lived with so long and hated so much) hit my nose. . . . The tired stale smell of cheap liquor and cheap love. But right then I didn't much particular, as long as Millie went with it. I just wanted my mother to put her arms around me (which she did once in a while on Sundays) and hold me enough to make the ache in my gut go away.

Millie and I lived in two rooms over the Maple House restaurant. This was home, and for all my sixteen years in Cornwall, Vermont, it was all the home I ever knew. One room was a kitchen, with

3

a table for eating and a cot where I did my sleeping. The other room was where I was right now, half on Millie's big double bed and half on the floor, and wondering the best I could about just what to do next. I could lay here all night and bleed to death. Or maybe make it down the same stairs I come up and crawl down the street to Doc Cushing's. In the shape I was in, that was going to be one long belly-aching crawl. But it sure preferenced bleeding to death. My life here in the town of Cornwall wasn't anything great, just being "Millie's boy." I'm not much, I thought, but I'm all I got.

What got me up and on my feet was a wagon. Under the window and down on the street, I heard the wagon start rolling; as if it had been there all the while, listening to me decide whether to let myself live or die. I tried to reach the window beside Millie's bed and call for help, but the window stuck like a brother and wouldn't open up right away. Before I loosed up the ice, the wagon had turned the corner by the hardware store and was plumb out of sight. All I saw was hoof tracks and wheel ruts in the snow.

My gut hurt like it was coming apart. Leaning on the windowsill, I wondered where my mother had went to, and also tried to study how I'd make it down the stairs. By walking, I decided. So I walked, doubled over, toward the kitchen. I'd a made it too, if I hadn't tripped over Millie.

She was sprawled all over the kitchen floor. The first part of her I touched was her arm. Even in the dark I knew it was my mother. No arm but hers ever wore so many bracelets, and she wore 'em day and night.

"Millie," I said. I almost called her "Mother," but it was too late for that. She never allowed me that, to call her Mother. It wasn't a boom for business in her line of work to have a boy my age. Not when Millie was still as pretty as she was. So I called her Millie, just like anybody else. That was the way she wanted it, and it was square with me. Millie's style of entertainment put bread on the table, and I was partial to eating.

My hand moved along Millie's arm until it felt the wet, gun-tore flesh. Her body was still warm; but there was no pulse. Her heart had stopped. When I knew she was dead, I just went cold all over, and started to shake a bit. Blood was everywhere, and I couldn't tell where mine began or hers quit. The one thought that crossed my brain was how thankful I was that the lamp wasn't burning. Even in the dark, I could tell that what was left of my mother wasn't a pretty sight to see.

I rested my head on her chest and felt like I was going to open up and cry. She smelled like she often smelled. I guess she'd spilled some whiskey on her dress. God, how I hated that smell.

5

"You're dead," I said out loud, almost like it was a question 'stead of an answer.

I couldn't believe it. And it bothered me that I wasn't all shook with grief, but I wasn't. Maybe it was because my own self was in such bad shape that I just couldn't handle any mourning. It wasn't the time for pity. I was a goner if I couldn't raise Doc Cushing.

My mother's body was lying in the path 'tween me and the kitchen door, so I crawled over her as fast as possible. It sure did hurt to move, and I began to ponder about how much blood I'd already lost . . . and also how much was left. I figured if it hurt a lot to crawl, that walking couldn't hurt much more. Using a kitchen chair under one hand and the table under the other, I got to my feet. Doubled over, but up. I opened the kitchen door and was just about to start down the stairs, when I heard the worst spooked-up noise you ever heard.

Millie's arm must of twitched about five times, and all her bracelets rattled. It was as if she was still alive and moving about the place. I don't know what made me say it, but the word was passed my lips with no thought behind it . . . like a question there weren't no answer to. It was a flinch, just like hers. I just said it straight out:

"Mother?"

2

Somebody was carrying me through the dark but I didn't know who. And cared even less.

Whoever it be was strong as all hell, as he was running with me in his arms. He was breathing real hard, but he didn't stop to ease it. He just kept on wheezing and packing me along through the snow. My head was hanging down as we turned in at the white gate of a picket fence. That was when I recognized the sign out front, and saw his name. I'd been to his place and seen that sign so many times I didn't have to read it.

> AUGUST TOBIN
> SHERIFF
> ADDISON COUNTY, VERMONT

"Easy, boy."

It was Gus Tobin's voice. He had a soft voice,

7

almost like music. Some of the men in Cornwall said that it was his voice that got him elected sheriff, and also made him the best man around at handling Morgan horses.

With his boot, Gus kicked the door open. We were in his office, and he whirled around as if he didn't quite know where to set me down. Lifting up his knee, he held me with it and with one arm, while his free hand swept the papers off his desk. The big desk was covered with papers and they all rattled to the floor. That's when Gus lied me down on his desk; and grunted, as if to say he was damn glad to drop his load. A lamp was at low burn in one corner of the office, and before Sheriff Tobin turned it up so he could recognize me, he spoke up.

"Who are you, boy?"

"It's me. Tit. Tit Smith."

"Millie's boy?"

"Yeah, Millie's boy. Gus?"

"Huh."

"I think I'm shot. And my—"

"Shot, beat up, or mule-kicked. Tit, you're so bloody I don't know where to start putting you whole again. Where's the hurt?"

"All over. But my—"

"Getting gunshot is like that. I know for a fact. But when you move, where's the sharp of it?"

"My belly."

"Here?" When his hand touched my gut, I almost kicked myself off his desk.

"I was trying to make it to Doc Cushing."

"You never would of, not in the shape I found you in."

"Gus?"

"Yeah."

"Millie's dead."

As I said it, I felt Gus's hand twitch, the hand that was trying its best to pillow my head. For a while he couldn't speak. "You sure? I thought I heard a shot."

"She's dead, Gus. And I'm going to be deader. Jesus, it hurts like a sonofabitch. Please, go fetch Doc."

"Doc's out of town. Went to Shoreham."

"I'm gonna die, Gus."

"No you ain't. Quit being a baby. All you took was probably one little old ball of lead. One dose. My guess is that it was a scatter gun. If'n you'd took the full of it, it'd cut you in half. Lucky you didn't."

As he talked, Gus was peeling off my coat and shirt. Real easy. He undid my belt and snaked my britches down. He went away for a minute and then come back with some rags and a crock of hot water. When I felt it I guess I jumped.

"Lie easy, Tit. You ain't hurt bad."

"What you gonna do?"

"Wash you off."

"I'm bleeding."

"You was. Not no longer. But don't fret on that. Blood always looks to be more than it is. A few drops'll color a whole shirt. You still got a bucket left in you, that is if you got the sense to lie still and let it cork."

"It's my belly. I feel I got a hole in me you could stanchion a cow in."

The warm water was washing me. It felt good, but every second I was feared that old Gus was going to touch that slug hole. When he finally did, I let out one hell of a yip.

"There it is," Gus said. "I can almost put my little finger in it."

He rolled me over on my hip for a bit while his hand rubbed along my backside, like it was searching for something. "It went in," Gus said, "but it sure didn't come out, lest it flew out your bunghole. You sure about Millie, your ma?"

"Dead."

"You real sure now?"

"Go look."

"I aim to. But first it's you that takes looking to. I can't believe it about Millie. I don't want to believe it. Why Millie? Some dirty, no-good—"

"I guess Millie wasn't much better," I said. Maybe, because I was hurting so much, I was piling blame on my mother for everything that happened.

Gus Tobin yanked his hand out from under my neck, and the back of my head hit the hardwood desk.

"Don't you say that, boy. Don't say nothing like that about your ma. What in hell do you know about Millie? I never let nobody talk about her like that. You included. Now keep that mean mouth of yours shut and bolted, and maybe I'll pull the lead out your belly."

"I'm sorry, Gus."

"You oughta be. Bad-mouthing your own ma like so, and her not even cold. Millie Smith was a lot of things in her time. Some bad and some good. The last few years . . . well, I guess it's all better not spoke of."

There was a sink in the next room, where Gus had got the hot water. I heard him washing his hands. Knowing that Gus would tend to my wound made me feel better. When he came back, he smelled clean—like strong brown laundry-soap —and the sleeves of his faded blue workshirt was rolled up near to the shoulder. His arms were thin and white, not very hairy. And they looked a bit pink where he'd rubbed himself dry with the muslin towel that he still had in his hand. Then he returned to his kitchen, and I could hear the rattle of tools in a drawer. Or spoons, like he was looking for stuff. I guess he found it, because after that he poured more boiling water on whatever it was.

"What's that?"

"A probe. And some needle-nose tongs."

"You going to dig out the slug that's in me?"

"I got to find it first. That's what a probe is for."

"Will it hurt?"

"It ain't exactly fun."

"Why don't we wait until Doc Cushing gets back from Shoreham?"

"Because he'll be there until midweek. His mare is lame and there's a smithy in Shoreham where Doc can maybe get her shoes reset proper. One of her hoofs went sore."

"I sure wish Doc was here. Christ!"

"Easy, son. Well, I don't. I seen that shaky old fart take a bullet slug out of me. The old butcher carved me up in small pieces, and it took him half the night to do it. Between you and me, I wouldn't let Doc Cushing cut a tail off a cat."

"God!"

"I found it. Sorry, Tit."

"You get it out?"

"Hell no, I didn't get it out. I just found the bastard."

Gus didn't know it, but he'd just used the one word that made me wince more than pain. Millie was an unwed woman. I'd been called "bastard" by more than one kid in the school. Long before

I even knew it meant a kid with a ma and no pa. And no real name.

"Here," said Gus, pulling the cork out a dusty bottle, "this here is brandy. Drink some."

I took a good pull on the bottle, and swallowed it down. "I'm on fire, Gus."

"More," said Gus. "Now you're afire, piss it out with one more gullet full."

So I took one more nip. It was real smarty, and I felt my whole head was burning up.

"Is that your first drink of brandy, Tit?"

"No, it's my last."

"How old are you? About fourteen?"

"I'm sixteen. Bloody mother of God! What the hell are you digging me with, a shovel?"

"I almost got it. Hang on, Tit. And bite on this pencil. Bite real hard, like it's what's hurtin' you and you aim to hurt it back."

Just as my teeth bit down on the big brown pencil that Gus put crosswise in my mouth, I felt something cutting my gut, and I felt like I'd just got ripped from belly to brisket. My hands grabbed the edges of Gus's desk, and for a few seconds I sunk a bit closer to crazy.

"I got it."

My mouth was full of pencil splinters, but it didn't much matter. It wasn't my tongue that was in agony but everything else sure was. I figured the real hurt was over when I heard Gus say that he'd got out the bullet. But I reckoned wrong. When he dug up the lead, that was just the start of it. I should of took a guess what the sheriff was fixing to do next when I heard him pop the cork once again on the brandy bottle. Then I knew why. Gus dumped the brandy into the hole in my gut, and that's when I really did it. I wasn't much of a hand at prayer, but I prayed to die. And that's when Gus held my head with both his hands, and held it tight firm against his shoulder.

"Tit, I don't cotton to see anybody take pain, man or animal. But let this pain remind you, boy. Your ma took pain worse than this when she bore you. And before she bore you, with no name to give you. And after she bore you, for sixteen year. Remember it, Tit Smith. Remember her hurt, just like your gut hurts now. And don't you never hurt no woman like somebody hurt Millie."

This was what Gus said just before the room went dark. Real dark.

3

"You awake, Tit?"

"Gus?"

"I'm right here."

"What time is it?"

"You going someplace?"

"How long have I been asleep?"

"Quite a while."

"It's morning."

"Sure is. A clear Monday morning."

Sheriff August Tobin was sitting in the ladder-back rocking chair in the corner of his bed chamber. Just under his chin, he held a tin cup of what smelled to be hot coffee in both his brownhide hands. I could tell he'd already been outdoors. One of his boots was up and rested across a small wicker stool. The sole was wet. And the other boot on the floor had a puddle of water around it, where the snow had melted off.

"Gus?"

"Yeah."

"You say Monday?"

"Sure did."

"What happened to Sunday?"

"You sleeped it off."

"I did?"

"Yep. Maybe I give you too much brandy. By the way, how's your gut?"

That was when I moved. Real careful at first, because I was so scared of the pain coming back. My hand went to my belly and felt the big cloth bandage that Gus Tobin had wrapped across my middle. My back was stiff. I was stretched out faceup on Gus's bed and under covers.

"I'm dying of thirst."

"Wouldn't wonder. Want some coffee?"

"Yeah . . . please."

Gus stomped off to the kitchen, and I just lay easy and looked at all the little chips of white paint that was peeling off the bedroom ceiling.

One of the chips was so curled up, it was just hanging by a corner. Looked like it was going to drop before the day was through. I yawned, and started to really wake up. Then my memory hit me. Millie was dead. And now I was just Millie's boy, with no Millie.

16

"Black?"

"What'd you say, Gus?"

"You take your coffee black? I got sugar."

"Sugar's fine."

"How much?"

"Lots."

"Want cream in it?"

"That'd be real good."

There was a pause before Gus finally said, "I'm all out of cream."

"Milk'll do."

"Hey! If'n I had milk, I'd of give you cream." Gus was smiling as he handed me a hot steaming tin cup of coffee. I scorched my mouth with the first gulp, just as I caught up the meaning of his joke. The coffee was good. Gus didn't skimp on sugar. But all the time I was drinking it, I couldn't get Millie out of my head. She was gone.

"Gus?"

"Huh."

"You been over there?"

"Over to your place? Yes, I took myself over. About an hour after I cut you open and pulled the lead. You was sleeping like a baby."

"I reckon you saw."

"I saw."

"How—"

"It weren't pretty."

"You got to promise me, Gus."

"Promise what?"

"You got to bring in the man who done that to Millie. Bring him to hang."

"You got my word."

"You'll hang him?"

"I'll bring him in, Tit. But I won't hang him until a jury gives the nod. And when they do, it'll be my pleasure to help bust . . . his . . . neck. I pledge to you, boy, that I'll knot his rope tight and personal. He'll feel every bristle on that rope."

"Gus?"

"Yeah."

"Did you make . . . arrangements? You know, for—"

"For burying? Yeah, I talked to Lucas Mix. We took the remains to the vault. Ground is froze, so we can't bury her until spring."

"What about a funeral?"

"Up to you, Tit."

"Me?"

"You're next of kin."

"Reckon I am."

"I don't know no one else. Leastwise, not here in Cornwall."

"What do you mean by that, Gus?"

"Nothin'."

Gus Tobin always did that. He'd say half of something that might be important, then he'd clam up and leave the rest unspoke. I felt like yelling at him, and finally did.

"Tell me, Gus!"

"Easy, boy."

"Tell me, damn you."

"You know, Tit . . . when you get mad, that red hair of yours looks even redder."

"Tell me."

"Just gets redder and redder, like your head was on fire. You got the reddest hair I ever seen on man or fox."

"Gus, there's a mean streak in you."

"There's a mean streak in everybody. There's one in me, and that's for sure. I was mean to you just now, because—"

"Because what?"

"Tit, some things are hard to say straight out. I was cussed on account that I put blame to you for lots of things."

"What things?"

"Things no fault of yourn. And I guess my mean streak is still making you answer up to the sin of somebody else."

"You mean Millie?"

"Yeah. You know that. You knew about Millie and me."

"Guess so."

"It was some time back. Years ago, when your ma first come to Cornwall."

"What was she like? Was she pretty?"

"Sort of. But I don't guess Millie Smith were what you'd call a pretty girl. But she had something. She had a special way about her, about the way she walked and held her head."

"Why did Millie come here to Cornwall?"

"You."

"Me?"

"Yeah, you. She was carrying you in her belly, without no husband at her side. She lived in the hotel, at the Cornwall House, at first. Then she moved to Ellie's."

"What was that?"

"Ellie's? Well, some said it was a boardinghouse, and some said no it weren't. It was run by a woman named Ellie Newell. Or maybe it was Nowell. I disremember. It don't make a nevermind what her name was. It was all a time ago, too long to give a rat's ass about."

"What did my ma do at the boardinghouse?"

"Worked."

"At what?"

"At saving up enough jack to lie abed and have you, that's at what."

"So I got born. Then what?"

"Then the town got holy about it, just like it was their business."

"How?"

"Millie used to go to church, and some of the righteous up and asked her not to attend no more. On account she had a redheaded kid out of wedlock, and nobody knew who sired it. I don't guess there was a one of 'em who wouldn't miss supper in order to talk about Millie, and to speculate as to who your pa was that sowed the seed."

"Who was he?"

"What makes you think I know?"

"You know plenty, sheriff. Plenty that you shut up about. Who is he?"

"Beats me."

"Is it you, Gus?"

"Sometimes I wish I was your pa. Lots of times."

"But it could of been you."

"I 'spose. But it weren't me."

"How do you know?"

"All I know is, your ma was leastwise two months' gone, and maybe more, by the time she come to Cornwall. She got here, I recall this much for sure, just before Thanksgiving. The year was 1881, or was it '82? No matter. Anyhow, you got yourself born the following Easter, near the end of April. When's your birthday?"

"Millie never told me, Gus."

"I recollect. It's the twenty-two of April."

"You sure?"

"I'm sure. April 22, 1882."

21

"Gus?"

"Yeah."

"Who's my pa?"

"Tit, I honest don't know."

There was still a swallow of coffee in the tin cup. But I didn't care. My arm just cocked back and throwed the cup at Gus Tobin hard as it could. It was like my arm did it all by a lonesome, without me. I throwed it real hard at close range, and it hit Gus in the face. High up, and right on his cheekbone. It bounced off his face, and hit the wall. The cup was all the way behind his rocking chair when the tin finally stopped clanking.

"Pick it up."

Gus's voice was stone cold and as even as the spine of a skinning knife. He didn't repeat the order, and he didn't have to. I knew if I hadn't dragged myself off that bed and picked up that cup, that Gus Tobin just might boot my butt from hell to breakfast. So I fetched the cup doubled over and hurting. But I weren't bleeding none. I took it to the kitchen, pumped some cold water into it, and set it bottom-up on the drainboard by the sink. Somehow I walked to him and stood straight.

"I'm sorry, Gus."

"Forget it. Get your bare feet back into bed."

Gus wiped the streaks of coffee off his face with a red bandana, stuffing it back into the back pocket of his jeans when he was through.

"I just figured you know who my pa is, that's all. I figured you know and won't say. Guess I was wrong, Gus."

"Maybe so," Gus said. "And maybe not."

4

Gus was wearing his specs.

He always wore them to read in and do his papers; which he was now doing, sitting at his desk. It was the same desk I just got through spending a passel of hard times on, and it was one spot I didn't hanker returning to for another dose of Gus Tobin's doctoring.

"What you doing, Gus?"

"Working."

"At what?"

"At all the blessed-Mary paperwork and red tape that some durn fools who run the State of Vermont invented to torment a county sheriff with."

"Oh."

"And what might I ask are you doing?"

"Nothing."

24

"Just like there's nothing that wants did. Tit, I think you got mixed up somewhere with a hound dog. You might as well learn it early. Lazy folks just don't go nowheres. Except to bed. That's why people who are living on the County have so many cussed kids that they expect the rest of us to feed."

"Yeah," I said, "guess you're right. I'm well enough to help."

"Well, I been hand-feeding you for three days. And not once have I heard you offer to lift a finger. You weren't hurt that bad."

"Sorry, Gus."

"Sorry ain't enough."

"What can I do?"

"For a start, you can stop asking such a tomfool question. You can *see* things to do. Out in the kitchen, there's a sink full of crockery that needs washing. You dirtied half those dishes, and you're nigh to mended. So at least go out there, roll your sleeves up, put on an apron, and be a man."

I looked to see if Gus was smiling. He wasn't. He sure got mean at times, but he was honest to live with. Since I got shot three days ago, I'd stayed here with Gus. I never had it figured for a final arrangement, for always. It was just that I didn't want to go back over to the Maple House restaurant. Not after what happened. I didn't know where else to go, so I just stayed with Gus.

"You aiming to stay on in Cornwall?"

"No," I said.

"Where you aim to go?"

"Now that my gut is on the mend, I guessed I might sort of head out on my own."

"Head out where?"

"Bennington, maybe. I always wanted to see that place. Or maybe even to Boston."

It was just a lot of big talk. Gus gave a snort to say he didn't believe it neither. I didn't even know my way out of town, say nothing about Boston. I filled the kettle to boil some hot water for the dishes. I stood at the potbelly and waited for it to boil. It took its own sweet time about it. But there was no sense in pestering Gus when he was working his papers. Soon there was a sink full of hot soapy water and the dishes got did. By me.

There was a window above the sink that looked to the back yard. The kitchen lamp was turned up full, and so was the one near Gus's desk. There was light on the fresh snow as it built up on the neat pile of firewood that Gus had split for his cook stove. The wood was all butt-pointed toward the house, and all you could see was a lot of yellow moons. And squares, where it'd been split. Inside every snowflake it looked like there was a tiny speck of silver. December, I thought. What a month to try to leave Cornwall. But there was no staying. I didn't want to live with Gus, and it was plain that he didn't want it either. He liked me well enough. But he'd lived alone too long, too many lonely years to all of a sudden be a nursemaid to a sixteen-year boy. It would ask too much of Gus, and I liked him too much to ask.

Besides, when he looked at me, it wasn't me he ever saw. It was Millie. Sometimes his eyes went sort of soft, as if he liked me because he liked her. Then my crop of red hair would remind him that I was hers and not his. The red hair sure didn't say August Tobin. It said some other man. I figured it all out as the dishes got scrubbed. There was me, the son of a woman he loved and a man he probably hated. Perhaps he hated that man too much to even say his name. Or too much to ever want to *know* his name.

Outside the sink window, the snow kept coming down—as it had now since Saturday night. In just the short time it took to scrub the dishes, the snow seemed to be a deeper, colder white.

"Tit?"

"Yeah, Gus."

"Ain't you even going to ask?"

"Ask what?"

"Didn't you ever ponder why I never went to track down the man that shot your ma?"

"I figured you would when the time was right. I don't guess he'd ever get far in this snow."

"Not very. Whoever it was, boy, my guess is that he's still in town."

27

The dishes were done, dried, and stacked away in the cupboard. Now I was working the very last chore, the big black skillet that Gus used to cook our supper. He'd fry pork and potatoes in the same old black "spider," as he called it. It sure was good, whatever he fried up.

"So you guess that he's still in town, Gus?"

"Sure do. What's your guess?"

"My guess is that he drives a wagon."

"How come you never mentioned that before?"

"I just now recalled it."

"A wagon, huh? Tell me more."

"Well, it's all sort of foggy in my head. But it's clearing up. It was right after I got shot. I figured the same shot that notched me also killed Millie."

"Go on, keep telling."

"I was over at the barn dance."

"So was every soul in town."

"Let me get to it, Gus. I was coming home from the dance. Must of been around midnight. Anyhow, the dance was most over. I'd asked a girl if she'd dance the next square with me, and she said—"

"God, boy—is all this pertaining?"

"It's all leading up to coming home by myself, up the front stairs. I saw a wagon behind the restaurant."

"Was the restaurant open?"

"No. Gus, you know as good as me that the

28

Maple House is never open until midnight. Not even on Saturday night."

"That's a fact."

"So as I come up the stairs I heard talking."

"Who?"

"As I got closer, it didn't sound like Millie. I usually don't come home when Millie's got company. You know."

"I know."

"If I do, I just creep real quiet up the front stairs and into the kitchen and don't ever go near the bed chamber or the back stairs."

"Keep going."

"Well, I heard some talking. Somebody sounded like they was crying. There weren't a lamp burning, so I didn't want to walk in on 'em. But since I figured it might be Millie crying and taking on, I wanted to see who was giving her grief."

"Go on."

"As I opened the door, I didn't see nobody. The curtain to her bedroom was drawed shut. All I heard was the start of a scream, and then the shot. It was the loudest gun blast I ever did hear."

"Just one?"

"Yeah. Why?"

"I want to know if there was two quick shots. Then we'd know for sure to hunt a man with a double barrel."

"That's pretty smart, Gus."

"I keep telling ya." Gus tapped his head with a finger.

"Well, that's all. Except the boots."

"What kind of boots?"

"Big heavy boots. Gus, I got a hunch."

"Then hunch."

"I got me an inkling in my mind's eye. I can just see them boots. Big and flat-heeled, like I can almost see the man that wore 'em. He's a big man, Gus. Big and heavy and mean, and he carries a shotgun."

"Not no more, he don't."

"He don't?"

"Listen, Tit. If you shot a woman, and you was snowed in and couldn't leave town, what would you do?"

"Hide."

"Think, boy, and study on it. Wouldn't it be easier to just hide a gun than hide a two-hundred-pound man?"

"I'd get rid of the gun."

"You sure would, boy. And fast. Where's the slug I picked out of you?"

"Here, in my pocket."

"Look at it."

"It's just a little old ball of lead."

"What does it tell you?"

"It ain't very big. No bigger than the tip of my

little finger. Looks like it come from a very small gun."

"Or one hell of a granddaddy big one."

"How so?"

"When I went over to your place that night, after doctoring you, there must of been a dozen holes in that room. So I took out my knife and dug one, just one, out of a wall timber."

Gus reached into his pocket, pulled out something, and tossed it to me. I caught it, and it was another ball of lead.

"Now you got two," Gus said. "You got one the hard way. But take a closer look. Ever see shot such as that?"

"No. Where's it from, Gus? Where do they pour lead like that?"

"Don't know. But your ma sure stopped a full load."

"She ought to be proper rested, Gus."

"She ought. Back home, too."

"Where'd she come from, Gus?"

"West of Larrabee."

"Where would that be, her rightful home?"

"Ticonderoga."

5

Dear Gus

I ben thinking. And I am going to
~~Tye~~ Ticonderoga. Please tell Mr. Mix when
I come back we can bury Millie proper. Gus
thank you for all you dun. But I just
got to go now that the snow is stoped.
I got to find out who my pa is. I wish
it was you. By the time you reed this
I will bee out of Addison County. If I
make it to ~~Tic~~ Ticonderoga I wil write
a leter. I am greatful for what you dun.
Even if it still hirts.

Your freind
Tit Smith

I leaned the note against the sugar bowl on the kitchen table that had red-check oilcloth on it. I was real quiet, so's not to wake up Gus. I only took what was mine, no more. Just the clothes I wore.

I ran across the street to the Maple House restaurant. The clock in the window said that it was almost two o'clock in the morning. Good. It would give me a plenty head start if Gus was a mind to follow. But he had to wake up first. And seeing as he didn't get himself to bed until after midnight, I had him beat. I was sleeping when I heard him and another man come in. They made hot tea in the kitchen and talked some. I figured that Gus helped him steam his stallion. But the old boy didn't make it. I couldn't make out who the other man was. His voice was sort of broke up, on account of he thought plenty of that stud horse. He gave thanks to Gus and took leave. When Gus dragged his own self to bed, it sounded like he was just wore out. He didn't even wash.

Early in the night, before Gus come home, I looked at the papers on his desk. One was about me, so I read it. It was a form that Gus was making out for the County Farm. It had my name on it. I guessed I would be sent there, as it was all legal and proper. Gus had wrote "no mother, no father, no known kin," in the space that was for REMARKS. The rest was just a lot of law talk, which didn't mean a thing. Gus had filled it all out. Then something must of made him mad, because the paper was all crumpled up—like he'd throwed it away. And later changed his mind. It had words on it like "pauper," almost in every part. Gus didn't write them. They was already there.

Just before I quit reading it, something that really mattered caught my eye. It was in the space where you were supposed to fill in the full name of the most recent living relative. That was where Gus had wrote a name and then rubbed it out. I took the petition over to the light, turned up the wick wheel, and held the paper up against the lamp chimney. I could read it! The name that Gus had wrote in and rubbed out was *Millicent Sabbathday*.

It give me a start to read it. My heart was beating and beating away. For a minute it was like being God, and looking down from above and seeing Tit Smith all naked and fresh-born. It felt real odd, like knowing what you were never meant to know. I kept saying the name over and over. Millicent Sabbathday. And because of me, she come to Cornwall over sixteen years ago and said she was Millie Smith. So I was half Sabbathday. So far, so good. It didn't help much with the other half. I kept looking at the rubbed-out name. It was like I knowed Millie as a girl. A young girl in trouble, who had run away to protect her family and to give birth to a bastard son.

With the tip of my finger, I touched the rubbed-out place. My hand got the shakes doing it. It was like I was reaching back sixteen years to 1882 and saying hello to my mother. She wasn't Millie any more. She was my mother, Millicent Sabbathday. It sounded so decent. A clean name. When I got back to Cornwall, I would tell Mr. Lucas Mix that I wanted a marker for her grave. Not just wood. It would be marble. Good Vermont marble that was as polished as meat, and it would have her name on it. Millicent Sabbathday. And I'd have a preacher say words. There would be dignity and respect for her, as right as the earth.

Over the restaurant, I moved real quiet. There wouldn't be nobody downstairs, but I moved soft just in case. Cal Short sometimes had a gal in the kitchen late at night. I used to hear the two of them giggling and carrying on. One night she gave him a bad time and they tipped over the rack that held all the copper pots and pans. You never heard a racket like that in your life, leastwise not in the middle of the night. Like churchbells. Must of woke up half of Cornwall. I figured the other half was under the quilts and didn't care. So just in case Cal was sparking a gal down in the restaurant, I moved like a guilty cat.

What I was there to do was packing, such as it was. I had an old kitsack that said U.S. Army on it. It was a real prize thing to own. A soldier (who stayed the night with us) left it behind. My mother said I could have it. So that was what I was packing.

We had a Bible and I took that. I can't tell why because I don't know. It wasn't like I was a regular reader of the Bible. I hadn't even cracked it. But it just seemed like the kind of thing that ought to go along. I added some spare stockings and underclothes, a shirt, half a bar of soap, a comb, a muffler (which I wound around my neck), a pencil, and a picture of my mother in an oval amber frame. It was taken when she was a young girl. I kissed it, then rolled it up real snug inside my extra shirt, the blue one. (I was wearing my gray shirt.) Then I stuffed the shirt with the picture inside down into the kitsack, buckled down the flap, put the pack on my back, and was ready to go.

There wasn't any food; except a can of coffee, half a tin of oatmeal, and three apples. I took it all. The last thing I grabbed was my hunting knife, which I shoved into my right boot. Gus Tobin said that was the place to knife-carry, and I figured the sheriff ought to know. Gus knew about all there was.

Just as I left, I turned to have one more look at the place. Something on the floor hit my attention. I bent over and picked up a yellow candy wrapper, twisted in the middle to give it wings like a butterfly. It smelled sweet. I wondered whose it was, as Millie never ate candy. Stuffing it into my coat pocket, my elbow knocked off a frying pan that

36

was on the edge of the sink. The noise it made in the dark of that kitchen could of woke the dead. Maybe not the dead, but it sure woke up Cal Short and his woman. Providing they was asleep.

"Hey! Who's up there?"

"Cal," I heard her say in a whine, "keep your mind on kissing."

"Be quiet, Agnes. Let me listen."

"I won't be quiet. I didn't come here to listen."

I recognized Cal's voice for sure; and the second time she spoke up, I knew who was keeping him company. Agnes Cratch. She worked at the Maple House (where Cal Short was the dishwasher) as a waitress. Agnes was well known around town. Some of the older boys at school called her Agnes Crotch. I reckoned I knew why. She and Cal must have been really having a good old him-an'-her downstairs, and I sure hated to disrupt such a worthy ritual. Cal Short was a regular kind of fellow who'd slipped me more than one slab of apple pie on the house (on the Maple House) so I didn't cotton to see a good man cheated. Especially seeing as Agnes was so bent on Cal's getting his full measure of merriment.

I would of gladly swapped places with Cal Short. Let him go to Ticonderoga; and me, well I'd just take his place down in the kitchen with Agnes. I'd seen her legs, and they were really something worth looking at. Not that Agnes came right up and showed 'em to me. Oh, no. But I was cleaning out the backroom of Rundle's Drygoods when Agnes come back to try something on that she liked to buy. She pulled her petticoats up, to get at some snap or hook that she didn't find easing her, and that was when I saw her legs. With nothing on 'em, even up above her knees. Her thighs were so round and white, just like twin loaves of soft, warm bread.

When it was quiet again, I walked down the back stairs on tiptoe, and out into the cold night air. The stars were out, and it was a good night to head west. I wasn't the first soul to leave town in a westerly way. Seems like lately, everybody was headed that direction—Ohio, Missouri, Kansas, and all the way to California. Someday I'd go too. But for now, I just whispered along in the night, watching my breath come out in gray curly plumes of steam. And listening to the music of my boots as they crunched the crisp dry snow, as I walked out of Cornwall, Vermont . . . heading out to find a pa.

And I was going to find who I really was, instead of being Tit Smith.

6

I had me a plan.

You got to be a fool to just head out into fifteen miles of wilderness without one. So I figured that if I walked a good pace and trotted some I could make the eight miles from Cornwall to Shoreham by sunup. At least by middle of morning, I'd make it to Sam's and beg a breakfast.

Sam Callum used to live in Cornwall, but moved his family to Shoreham. Sam was a farrier whose place of business had been on the main street in Cornwall, just beyond the livery stable. Next to a livery was always a good place for a smith to set up shop. There was plenty of horses that took shoeing, and Sam was the man to do it. I tried once to hammer a shoe. It was heavy work, and made my arms ache. Sam said I was too short for his anvil. A good smith always works an anvil that's knuckle high, as your hand hangs down.

His smithy was where I used to hang around some, on days when I didn't want to go home and barge in on what was intended to be private. Not only that, Sam always had a few pennies in his pocket for odd jobs that needed doing. Sometimes it was paring down a hoof, or just stroking the nose of a horse while Sam pulled out a twisted nail from a pulled-up hoof. Sam was a good blacksmith. He'd always wash off the frog of a hoof with cool water and then wipe it dry to see if the horse was sound. He could tell a lot about an animal by just picking up one hoof. So could I. I learned it working for Sam. He liked to pare the hoof back enough to let the "frog jump" as the horse's foot took its step— to make sure the frog soaked up the shock.

"Always shoe hot," Sam said, "and trust not a man who shoes cold. A mare is like a woman; she likes to put her bare feet into warm slippers."

As I walked along, remembering how Sam had said just that, it brought to mind the white rug that my mother had beside her bed. It was funny, how you could be alone on a cold night and think about a silly old white rug. Well, if it was soft whiteness I wanted, there sure was enough of it on that road. A few wagons had already broke the road to Shoreham, and I just walked in the tracks. One was real fresh. But as for the countryside, it was buried

40

under the white quilts of winter. It was like following a tiny trail across the top of a giant whipped-cream cake. There was no end and no beginning. Just snow and stars, as far as you could see. The black of the sky was as rich as the white of the snow.

A big white snowshoe hare run across the road so quick it made me jump. All I saw was the paddles of his hind feet as he disappeared over a rise.

There wasn't much to look at except the miles of gray ribbons left by wagon wheels, and sometimes the sharper ruts made by the runners of a cutter. But the sky was bigger. Heaven sure was grander than Earth. It was so peaceable, like all Vermont was praying that Tit Smith would make it to Shoreham and beyond. The only noise was the squeak of the snow as it packed under my boots. But it weren't quiet long.

"Woooooo—yoo—yoo—yoo—yip—yip—"

I stopped walking. It was a cold night, but in less than a couple of seconds, I was a wash of sweat. It was either timber wolves or coydogs and I didn't care which, as I figured both were sorry news. It sounded again, coming from the black, pine-thick ridge to my right. For me, it was either turn back and head home to Cornwall, or keep going. The third time they howled, it come from behind me. Closer this time. So I ran for Shoreham, still a good five miles away.

God, how I ran. Until the cold air burned my lungs, and long after both my legs felt like if they stopped they'd stop for keeps. It was crazy, but I started counting my steps as I ran. I'd get to a hundred and start over, trying not to think about the weight of the kitsack that was bouncing on my back like it was of a mind to drag me down. Each of my boots weighed like it was filled with rocks. When I finally tripped and fell forward on one knee, I just couldn't get up again.

But they weren't running. They bugled again, and they weren't any closer than before. And I hadn't pulled away. No, they wouldn't run. They'd trot. Just trot all night and all day, waiting for a deer or a man or a stray cow to fall over from fear, or to just fall over when its heart stops.

I couldn't see them. But I sure knew where they were. Behind me, trotting along on the road maybe a quarter mile back. And they sure knew where I was. I just kneeled in the wagon tracks and waited, with my hand on the handle of my knife. I waited for 'em to come. The road back home to Cornwall was straight from where I stood, straight for maybe a quarter mile where it bended away. So I waited with one knee in the snow, staring back at that bend in the road. Between me and the bend, there was a dip. Other than that, I could see back for a quarter mile, on account there was so much moon.

They came. Around the bend I saw the black

shapes moving along real steady on the white snow. They weren't in no hurry. Instead, they'd let me hurry. Hurry and hurry until I dropped over. They weren't gray, and so I figured 'em to be coydogs. Besides, nobody'd ever see wolves around Cornwall for ten years. It had to be coydogs. Just as mean as wolves, and Gus Tobin once said they was one bite meaner. Not quite as big, maybe. Gus had shot a coydog male and he hung dead at forty-four pounds. I weighed three times that much, I thought, and I got a knife.

I pulled it out of my boot. The blade was warm, where it'd lied against my leg and it felt good to hold. The handle was deer horn, and between the handle and blade there was a long two-ended hilt. It had been a present to me from Gus.

They were closer now. It looked to me like there was only a pair, probably a male and mate. The coydogs still trotted, their snouts pointed straight at me. If I could see them, sure as hell they could see me with them four yellow eyes that was getting bigger and bigger. The bigger shape was blacker than the other, and it be a good guess that the female was feral, a farm dog run off to go wild and mate wild and hunt wild.

It was odd how they'd picked up my scent on such a cold night. My boots couldn't of left a scent. Had to be more than just my boots and my breath. Looking down at my knife, I saw the answer.

There on the white hardpack snow was a tiny brown drop. Under where I was kneeling in the snow was maybe a dozen more. Most were brown. But one was fresh and bright red in the moonlight. I was bleeding. The coydogs had got a nose on it, maybe two mile back. Or even more. With all this snow driving the game underground, them two coys just had to be near to starved. And now they knew they had a warm-blooded meal, just ahead. They knew it cold, and there was no bother to run to it. Just trot, and follow the smell of the bloody drops on snow which had no smell. Trot, trot, trot.

As they come closer, the pair of coys were out of seeing, down in the dip of the road. Now was my chance. I got up and ran to Shoreham. I didn't know how far it was and maybe I'd never get there. But now that I'd got my breath back, I sure weren't going to sit on a road with my ass in the snow and wait on a brace of coys to offer up my throat to. If'n I was going to die, it was to bleed to death on the run. Not just calling it quits to a scurvy pair of coydogs. Hell with that.

"Sam! Sam! Sam!"

If only that big old blacksmith could hear me all the way to Shoreham. But I knew he couldn't. Sam Callum and his family were snug under quilts. My voice would be lost under the blanket of a Vermont wilderness. I yelled his name again and again, even though I knew Sam Callum's ear couldn't catch the call. It was still too far a piece from Shoreham. I sure weren't going to turn back into the teeth of them coys. All I could do was run and don't quit. And keep yelling for some lonesome soul who just might be nearby enough to hear. That, and to make sure my legs didn't stop.

So I ran. My legs couldn't stop running, and my head couldn't stop thinking. I said good-bye to Millie, to Gus, to Cal, and to the few people I like in Cornwall. My head was thinking and talking all the while. It was the last chance it got, so it was going fast—like my body. Run, run, run, Tit Smith. Run until you bleed to death, and keep running. I knew now what them words mean:

On a dead run.

7

When somebody pulls the trigger of a real genuine Montgomery Ward "Texas Ranger" long-barrel 12-gauge shotgun on a quiet Vermont road on a cold, clear December night, it sings out a handsome noise. Soft as a cannon.

First I thought one of my ears had got blowed off, because the roar of that gun was right next to my head. The only other thing I knew was that my left cheek was cold. Lying belly-down in the road, my face was snug to the hardpack and my cheek froze to ice.

BAM! . . . bam . . . bam . . .

The gun spoke again, and the echo of it bounced off the hills until it finally got swallowed up in the night. Whoever was shooting that gun was lying beside me in the snowy road. I heard the gun break

46

open and a fresh shell get thumbed into the breach, followed by a click as the gunman latched it whole again. Whoever he was, he sure didn't believe in drawing a bead or gentle-squeezing a trigger. He was just load and fire.

BAM!

My eyes were closed. But wanting to see who it was bad as I wanted, it was still hard to open my eyes. They wanted to sleep. So I just kept my cheek hugging snow, and smelling the smell of the burned-up saltpeter that come from the gun. My face was so cold, and yet my belly was red hot.

BAM!

"Die, you four-foot devil."

The voice was a strong voice, and those five words spoke that the owner of such a voice won't about to take nothing from nobody. Not charity. Not scorn. And when it spoke again, I knew I was in fair company.

"That's the last of that hungry rascal."

"There's two," I said, trying to raise up my face off the cold.

"Two? Two, my busted butt. There's closer to a half dozen."

"Two," I said, trying to get my eyes to open.

"In the shape you're in, sonny, you oughta got more blessed chores to do than count dead coys. Can you sit up and take notice?"

I felt the strong arms roll me over, and hold up my head. Trying hard to sit up, I finally did it. The person who held me was a woman.

"Good," she said.

I couldn't see very well. Everything was a bit on the cloudy side, as if the moon hid. But when I looked up into the sky, there it was—a big wafer of silver, like you could almost reach up and take a bite of it. Then I turned to look into another big round face, owned by the woman who held me. She was a big woman. Wearing no hat, her blonde hair was free, even though she wore it in two blonde braids as stout as bull ropes.

"What's your name, boy?"

"Smith."

"Well, that's safe enough."

"Safe enough for what?"

"Meaning," she said, "when a kid runs away from home, it'll always handle itself by Smith."

"Mine really is Smith. My name is Tit Smith."

"*Tit?*"

"It's short for Titmouse. When I was a baby, I was on the small side. I don't partial to it much, either to the long or the short of it. Who are you?"

"Call me Fern," she said, getting up on her feet. "Fern. Now ain't that one pip of a name for a lady of my girth? I guess my ma had a hanker for me to come up to be willow and lace, like a fern. And look at me. Almost six foot tall, and nigh to a hundred and a half heavy. I look about as much like a fern as you do a tit. You and me, we're a realsome pair." Fern laughed.

"We sure are."

"Why in the name of holy are we talking here like it was noon on summer? Get up."

"I don't know like I can."

"Try."

I got up on my feet, but if'n Fern hadn't of put her arm round me, I'd a gone down again.

"Feeling loony?"

"Yes'm."

"Lean on me. Now walk."

"Where to?"

"To my wagon. I got two mules just around the bend in the road that hate the bay of coydogs worse'n you do. Lucky for you I pulled 'em up short when I heared you yelling."

As she spoke of coydogs, I looked back down the road toward Cornwall. I could see three black shapes that were lied in the wagon tracks, not moving. One carcass was less than twenty feet away. It's face was sort of gray, with a red-brown body. From between the ears, there was a line of black hair that followed the spine and into the thick, stubby tail. Under the mean jaws was a creamy white throat. The mouth was open, and the tongue looked like it had been halfway torn out as it hung down with its tip to the bloody snow.

"Green Mountain coydogs," snorted Fern, "are big and mean. I seen coyotes out in west Kansas that look like mice beside them three. Vermont's got the biggest and meanest coys I ever see. Twice the heft of the western breed, or this ain't a shotgun. What you holding in your hand, boy?"

"Knife. It's mine."

"Nobody said it weren't. Come on, we'll cut you a fur piece."

Fern and me, we walked to the big coy. She took the knife out of my cold fingers and with one stroke cut off the coy's tail. It was thick and bushy and soft, as she tossed it at me. She wiped the knife off on the dog's body and handed it back to me. I shoved it down aside my right leg. And so with Fern carrying her gun in one arm and me in a half-tote under the other, we rounded the road to the backside of Fern's wagon. One of the mules turned its head as we come close, and the eyewhites wanted to know if I was coy or boy. The mule's nose-holes were pumping in and out, straining to get a whiff of what we were.

"Easy, girls," Fern said, helping me up on the wagon seat. "Easy. It's only me and a stray we just picked up. Tit Smith, meet Jack and Jenny. Real names are Jacqueline and Jennifer, and them two is about the shyest mules this side of hellsgate, so mind your manners."

"Yes'm."

"Well, girls. Let's make Shoreham."

The wagon yanked forward. Slipping off my kitpack, I let it sink behind me under the boot of Fern's wagon. I tried to keep my eyes open, but couldn't. Like it was all gray, even the mules which I knew were brown. The last thing I saw was Fern's big foot resting on the brakearm. Maybe I just blacked out. When I come to, Fern had me lying back inside the wagon boot, with something soft under my head. Beside me was the biggest cookstove I ever saw.

"Tit, you should of told me, boy."

"What happened?"

"You're bleeding."

My hand went inside my coat to my gut which was all hot and sticky wet.

"I know."

"What from?"

"A gun wound. But the lead is out."

"Son, let's pull off your britches."

"No, no. Got to get to Sam's. Got to get to Ticonderoga. I got to get me to a doctor." My head was rolling from side to side like it couldn't lie still.

"You are one lucky boy," I heard her strong voice say, like it was a mile away. "Now you yank down them britches or I'll do it for you and break buttons doing it."

"But you're a *lady*. I need a doctor."

"Wrong, boy. I'm no lady. Never was . . . but Fern Bodeen *is* a doctor."

8

"You better?" Fern asked.

"I guess so. I must of dropped off to sleep."

The wagon was still rolling through the snow, and I was still lying down under the cover of the wagon boot. Fern had her backside to me as she set the seat with the reins.

"Fern?"

"I'm listening."

"Are we to Shoreham yet?"

"Shoreham? We cut through that burg an hour back."

"No. Oh, no."

"You want to get out and go back?"

"Maybe I better."

"Up to you. Whoa, girls!"

As the wagon stopped, Fern turned around to look at me. Pulling off a mitten, she put a big cool hand on my brow. Then held it against my cheek.

"Tit, I don't much feel like carting you back to Shoreham. And I got doubts that Jack an' Jenny want to either. But I can't let you go back by yourself."

"Where you headed, Fern?"

"Cross lake."

"Cross lake from where?"

"Larrabee."

"Is that place much more than a holler from Ticonderoga?"

"On the way. You'll be in Ti by morning. Jack an' Jenny know it's downhill all the way to Lake Champlain. Besides I heard you yellin' about Ticonderoga, so I just thought I'd let you sleep yourself there."

"I was figuring on seeing Sam Callum."

"Where's he at?"

"Back in Shoreham. I wanted him to stake me to some foodstuffs. At least some breakfast. Then I'd move west."

"West to Ti?"

"Yes."

"If a breakfast is all you need, we'll take one at the Burleigh House in Ticonderoga. Best breakfast you ever ate. It'll be my treat, but you got to earn it."

"Earn it?"

"Yes, earn it."

"How?"

"Get your arse end up out of them blankets, climb up on this here seat and finger the ribbons. It's my turn for shuteye."

"Sure will."

I got myself up on the seat, and Fern handed me the reins. Then with a grunt or two, she took my place inside the wagon boot and out of the wind. As she put her head down, she let out a big sigh.

"Fern?"

"I'm asleep. You drive."

"That's just it. I never drove mules before."

"You ain't doing it now. Them two is taking you. Jack knows the way. Jenny's a mule who goes where Jack goes. And my Jack is one smart hinny."

"What's a hinny?"

"Most mules is of a male ass and a mare. Jack's old man was a stallion and her ma was a she-ass. That's a hinny."

"Oh."

"Now keep your wits. It's only five mile from Shoreham to Larrabee. Six at most. And then Ticonderoga is only two mile more. Just head for Larrabee."

"Where's that?"

"Cross lake from Ti. Now button up and let me sleep. Just follow my girls."

Fern Bodeen was asleep in the next breath.

Leastwise, there weren't no sounds from back there under them blankets. So I just sat that hard seat and hoped "the girls" were bound for Larrabee. If it really was true that Jack knew the way, I was grateful that one of the three of us had some smarts. Maybe it wasn't Jenny. But it sure wasn't me.

What in hell was I going to do in Ticonderoga? That'd take some answering, and Fern was sure to ask. Well, I'd just story it up. There was a paper mill in Ticonderoga. Everybody knew that. So I'd tell Fern Bodeen that I was to seek a job at the paper mill. The fact that I'd never even smelled a paper mill don't matter. Besides, she would probably just stop in Ti long enough to rest her mules. Jack and Jenny would be hungry too. It was one long haul to Ticonderoga, all the way from Shoreham.

But old Fern hadn't started in Shoreham. Where did she start from? Where'd she been? She was some sort of doctor, that was for sure. Or a darn good midwife. Too bad she wasn't in Cornwall the night I got shot. She could of popped that lead out easier than Gus Tobin. One thing sure, Fern would be asking about who put lead in my gut and who took it out. And when I tell her, maybe she'll haul me back to Gus. I'll have to study up a story that I got gunshot by mistake.

My hand felt inside my coat, down inside my

shirt, where Doctor Bodeen had stripped me raw, cleaned me up, and dressed my gut back up with a fresh white bandage. What Gus had on me had been just a change of rags. Fern's dressing looked like a doctor's work, not a sheriff's. Doctor Fern Bodeen. If'n she'd told me she was Teddy Roosevelt, I might of swallowed it quicker. Who ever heard of a lady doctor? When I thought about anybody being a doctor, it was always Doc Cushing. He was the only doctor in Cornwall. I guess Doc was pretty good at baby-bringing, as he had a passel to his credit.

But what was it Gus said? He told me that Doc did a slaughter on him, trying to pull lead. Carved poor Gus up for fair and warning. That was when Gus said he wouldn't let the old fart even cut a tail off his cat. And were I the cat, I wouldn't let Gus Tobin do it either.

I didn't know Fern from a back room. But in the hour or two that I'd seen her in action, I knew that there wasn't much in this old world that Fern Bodeen couldn't cut. She'd walk up to Satan and spit in his eye, reach in his mouth, grab his tail, and turn him inside out. That's what she'd do. She wouldn't take a backstep for even Old Ned. Not old Fern. But she was an odd duck. What in hell was she doing on the Shoreham road in the dark of the moon?

As Jack and Jenny moved forward without my

guidance, I looked back over my shoulder. Doctor Bodeen had rolled over. One of her big rope-thick blonde braids was across her face. In her sleep, her nose twitched as if the hair was worrying her. Leaning back on the wagon seat, I moved her braid off her face—real tender, so I wouldn't wake her up. As she rolled, she must of kicked the big yellow-check quilt off her. It took a good lot of tugs, seeing as Fern was lying on it, but I managed to get a purchase on one corner and tuck her in, so she'd been snug and warm.

"Much obliged, Tit."

When she spoke up, it almost made me jump out of my bandage; as I figured Fern was sleeping. But she must of woke up only that instance; because after them three words, there wasn't as much as a sneeze from her direction for the next five miles. Fern slept, and I just sat the seat and tried to figure out where Jack and Jenny were nosed.

It must of been Larrabee. Beside the road here was a sign with that very word on it. My lungs just filled up with night air and let out again. That sign that said Larrabee was a welcome thing to see, because I knew that Ticonderoga wasn't more than a mile or two beyond and I sure didn't cotton to following the wrong road. I had a notion that old Fern wouldn't take kindly to our missing a turn. So I kept myself awake by squeezing my knees together as hard as I could, whenever my eyelids took to drooping.

But I didn't squeeze hard enough. My eyes closed and my head nodded. As for "the girls," they headed for Ticonderoga. Smack dab through the hamlet of Larrabee, down the hill to the lake (as I later learned) and out onto the ice. There was only one trouble with Jack's plan. She was one smart hinny, and she was headed for the shores of York State and some Ticonderoga oats. But seeing as Fern was asleep back under the boot, which was piled high with lumps of everything, and me on the wagon seat, nobody told Jack and Jenny that they was headed toward an air hole.

When the wagon come to a stop, I jerked up my head. We weren't on a road anymore, and not even on land. I looked at nothing but a great big blanket of gray ice, all around. This had to be Lake Champlain, as nothing else could of been this big. And it was windy as hell. Not a snowflake on it.

I shook the ribbons, trying to get "the girls" to move forward. But they wouldn't budge. Them mules were shaking like a pair of hooked bullheads. Looking down, I saw why. Both the mules were standing ankle deep in water. And not two wagon lengths in front of 'em was one big air hole of black water. It was the mouth of Hell, and it went right to the bottom of Lake Champlain. Small

59

wonder them mules wouldn't take another forward step. Lucky they won't. The big cookstove in the wagon must have weighed a good four hundred pound.

Dropping the ribbons, I got down off the wagon seat and walked forward to where Jack and Jenny were tossing their heads in the air. I was walking in water that was ankle deep. One of my boots must of had a hole in it, because my left foot got real cold after one step. Up by the heads of the mules the water was a bit deeper. Grabbing a pair of reins under the chin of each animal, I tried to make 'em back up.

"Back up. Back! Back!"

But it seems like Jenny and Jack had other ideas. The water we stood in was cold as death, but them mules was boiling hot. Both were all sweaty and steaming, like they knew they was going to drown. Pulled down into that black water by the weight of the wagon. But they wouldn't back up. I tried to beat 'em back with my fists, but it was just like I wasn't hitting 'em at all. And I was hitting 'em hard on their noses. But they wouldn't move, and the water was climbing up almost to my knees.

Then I heard that dreadful noise, and it liked to make my heart stop. The ice split! So loud a split that the crack must of snaked from the south end of Lake Champlain to the north.

An ice crack, loud as lightning.

60

9

"What in hell . . .?"

Looking up between the heads of the mules, I saw the welcome sight of Fern Bodeen and all her bulk on the wagon seat, ribbons in hand.

"Fern! Back 'em up. Back 'em up!"

"Let go of those mules, boy. Don't nobody *back* mules. You got to turn 'em."

With me pushing on Jack, and Fern pulling the reins to bring her head around, the mules started to move. Jenny wasn't so sure she wanted any part of it, as it was her flank that had to wade almost knee deep in that icy water. But somehow, bit by bit and step by step, we managed to convince Jack. Once her head come round to look over her shoulder, back toward Larrabee and dry ice, old Jack decided that was the place for her. As the mules made their swing, the left forewheel of the wagon turned with them, rubbing against the wagon bin as it cornered as sharp as it was allowed. Its iron bracelet screamed against the wagon wood, a loud scraping scream—as if the wheel yelled out it could cramp no more.

Jenny didn't cotton to the howl of that wheel one bit. Up she reared, as the water poured from her forelegs. One of her hoofs caught me in the shoulder, knocking me backward into the surface water. In a second, I was heavy as lead and cold as death. Trying to yell to Fern, I opened my mouth; only to choke on the water. Somewhere under my boots, I knew I was standing on ice, but it didn't seem solid. It was like walking on jelly, thru water thick as jam. There wasn't any firm footing; and to bargain, my face kept going under.

"Tit!"

It was Fern yelling at me from somewhere, but I couldn't see her. The cold was all around me like coats and coats of heavy iron, and I started to feel like I couldn't move. And didn't care. The lake wanted me and it weren't to give me up.

"Here, boy! Look over here!"

I didn't know where Fern was, but I figured it best I find out. Twisting my head, I saw that she'd turned the wagon, but Jack and Jenny were still slipping and sliding on the wet ice. Everything seemed to be up in the air, as if it was higher and taller than I was.

"Tit!"

It was one hell of a hunk of luck. Just as I reached my hand up out of the water to yell to Fern, she threw me the reins. As they hit my hand, the whip and one rein lashed me right across the eyes. I was trying to grab it, but my fingers weren't working too quick. Fern was sitting in the foot cradle of the wagon seat, kicking the butts of them mules. When they started forward, I felt something snake along my neck and up over my lip. So I opened my jaws and bit it. My arms was so heavy and cold, they didn't seemed to want to help. They just couldn't swim up out of all that blackstrap-molasses water and get a purchase on that leather.

It sure was lucky I got good teeth. Reins that turn mules don't taste good. But right then, that flavor of old, worn cowhide was about the best thing I'd ever sunk my grinders into. My jaws just clamped on it and wouldn't let go—not even when the mules found footing and jerked me clear out of the water. It was a bit like being a caught fish. Or getting hung.

I couldn't get up. So I just lay there on the ice and didn't feel how cold I was. There really wasn't anything to feel; it was all beyond feeling. Lying on my backside, I saw the black velvet of sky; and all its stars, like snowflakes that would never come down.

Fern come.

She took hold on one of my boots and dragged me along the ice to where the wagon was. She got me up on my feet, slapping my face more than once, and up into the bin of the wagon. We were under the boot and out of the wind. All I remember is that there was ice all over me. All the water and all the wet was froze still and me in it. Instead of hair on my head, it was a hat of ice.

You wouldn't think a big woman like Fern Bodeen could move with any fast at all. But old Fern weren't no ordinary soul. Whipping out a knife, she cut off my clothes. The bandage, too. She wasn't wearing gloves and her hands must have been most to froze off, tugging on all that ice. Yet in less than a minute, I was naked as birth. Fern rubbed me all over with what looked like rag, but was too rough for cloth. It was either chammy or deerskin; because before she stopped buffing me, I reckoned there weren't no more hide on me to scrub.

Then she stuffed me into one-piece long underwear and rolled me up in the big yellow-check quilt. I figured the underwear on me was hers, on account there was enough room in it (besides me) for either Jack or Jenny. But when you're freezing to death, style don't count for much. Fern put the knife back inside a black leather satchel, and in the same motion pulled out a small bottle.

"Here," she said, lifting up my head with one hand as she spat out the cork, "this here is peach brandy. Made it myself, so I know it's good. One swallow will tie a knot in your gullet that won't bust loose for all day. Drink!"

Fern was right. As the brandy went down, I'd forgot what really good kerosene tasted like. It was a lot more brandy than it was peach. If she'd a brewed it out of boiled railroad spikes it couldn't of swallowed any worse. Fern kept the bottle upside down over my mouth; and like a fool, I kept on gulping. I never was much of a drinker. To some people, Fern's peach brandy might of been one hell of a rare treat. But far as I was concerned, it could of choked a roach.

Fern lit a lamp in the back of the wagon and held it down close to my face, so she could look into each of my eyes. Pulling out a clean towel, she rubbed my hair with as much spirit as she rubbed my hide.

"Tit," she said, "that hair of yours is so red, it wants to burn up. I never seen hair like that anywhere, except . . . it's not even red. It's orange."

Fern went on talking about somebody she knew once who had red hair, but I couldn't catch much more than a word or two. Never did hear the straight of it. I still had half of Lake Champlain in one ear, and the other half in the other. And I'd swallowed down a third half, if there was such a thing. Besides, the peach brandy had a kick worse than Jack or Jenny. It didn't make a nevermind what Fern Bodeen was saying. All of it was buried in the bubbles.

The wagon was moving. And it was starting to get light, though there wasn't a sun. Just a quiet, gray December morning. A long ways off I heard Fern urging the mules, and some other voices. But I don't guess I was awake enough to care. Folks were talking again. Somebody hauled me out of the wagon, quilts and all. Then up some stairs. I heard a man's voice.

"What ails this boy?"

"Well," said Fern, "only a few things. He's been shot, froze to death, run by coydogs, and drownded in the lake."

"He ought to be near dead."

"That boy ain't dead," said Fern. "He's dead drunk."

10

I sneezed!

Something was up my nose, and it sure was hot. But whatever it was, it weren't no hotter than the rest of me—because all of a once, I was just plain hot all over.

"It's only mustard," said Fern. "It ain't going to kill you. Just cook you raw. As my ma always said, there's nothing but a tub of hot mustard to melt a misery. The water's got to be near to boiling, and the mustard even hotter. So hot it'll raise a dead horse, or climb up into your backside so you whistle through your ears."

I was in a tub of water, and the tub was in the middle of a kitchen floor. Didn't know *whose* kitchen. My clothes were nowhere in sight, and I knew I was buck naked. But one thing sure, I had to get out of that mustard water or else burn to death.

"Close your eyes, Fern."

"Why?"

"I'm getting out. This water's so hot I can't stand another second of it. My hide's come off. So don't look."

"Don't look? Who, in the name of all that's good, do you think undressed you? Me, that's who."

"Where are my clothes?"

"Them? Some'll get washed, and some discarded. I never ran up against such a stink in my whole life. How long's it been since you peeled to the white-and-natural and took a bath?" As she spoke, Fern had her hand on my shoulder with more than a bit of heft.

"A week."

"Week, hell. Not even a mule could work up a stink like yours in only a week. You'd had to be at it longer than that."

"Maybe so."

"Fetch me that sponge, Amy."

"Here you are, Aunt Fern."

Suddenly I was cold again. I guess I just figured that there weren't nobody about in that kitchen except for me and Doctor Bodeen. And there I was, halfway out of that tub, with my bare bottom (probably beet red from half the mustard supply in Ticonderoga) pointing toward somebody I hadn't ever met up with. So there was one hell of a splash as I took cover under the boiling mustard. I felt as hot as a horseshoe, and it wasn't the yellow bath alone that did it. My face was redder than my butt.

"Mr. Smith," said Fern, "if you'll turn that red head of yours and stay put, I'd like to have you meet my niece—now that she's seen everything but your face. Miss Hallow, may I present Mr. Smith."

Even with mustard in both my eyes, Amy Hallow was the fairest girl I'd seen anywhere. Not that I'd been too many places (nowhere other than Cornwall) or seen many girls. She had hair the color of honey, and eyes as blue as a chicken gizzard. I had a mouthful of hot mustard water, and when I saw Amy Hallow, it got swallowed. If it tasted any worse than Fern's peach brandy, the difference weren't enough to take note of.

"Hello, Mr. Smith."

"Hello."

"Aunt Fern and I are glad to see that you are recovering."

"Thank you," I said. When it come to sparkling conversation with ladies, my tongue was pure poetry. Lucky for me, Amy could say it all.

"What is your Christian name, Mr. Smith?"

"Huh?"

"Your first name, what did you say it was?"

"My first name?"

"Yes. As mine is Amy, yours is . . .?"

Out of the corner of my eye, I could see Fern at the kitchen sink. Her back was to me. I didn't have to see that big face of hers to know she was enjoying all the sport. Because her big body was shaking, she grabbed a hold of the sink edge and hung on for dear life. But it didn't stop the rest of her from having a good time.

"Yours is . . .?" Amy said again.

"Tit."

Saying it made it sound worse to me than it did to her. It was the first time in my life that I promised myself that one day I'd be more than just Tit Smith. Naked in a tub of hot mustard water, with not a penny in my britches, I sure was off to a grand and glorious start.

"Your name is Tit Smith?"

"Yes'm," I said, keeping up the pace that I'd set earlier as a real tamer of wild words. If Amy weren't impressed by my bathing habits or my name, then I'd stun her with my oratory. By this time, she thought she was up against a second James Whitcomb Riley. Or maybe even the first.

"My aunt is always finding things and bringing them home."

"That's nice," I said.

"On her last trip, it was a baby crow. And we spent weeks trying to teach it to talk."

"Yeah?"

"How long do you suppose it will take us to teach you?"

It was now or never. My head was coming apart with a brandy hangover, and the hole in my gut burned so bad it felt as if the hot lead was still buried there. I guess I wasn't going to take any more guff. Not from Amy, not from anybody.

That was when I faced Amy, stood straight up in tub, stepped out of it and walked over to her. In front of me, I held nothing but a big sponge, just so she could see I was a redhead at both ends. I gave her a pinch on her pretty chin with my wet soapy hand, and answered her last question.

"Miss Hallow," I said, "not as long as it'll take to teach you manners."

11

Fern was standing with her fists on her hips, watching me put down the supper that she'd brung upstairs. Although it was hours back, I was still scorched from the mustard bath; but Fern made me get into bed "in the guest room." That's where I was eating, with the tray on my lap.

"What is this, Fern? It's right good."

"Tomato pie. And it ought to be good, since I made it."

"I confess I preference it over your peach brandy."

"Ever see a soul die with pneumonia?"

"No."

"Well, I have. Your one lucky boy you're alive and warm in a Ticonderoga goose-bed instead of froze-up for keeps. And I make darn *good* brandy."

"Fern, I sure do thank you for all you done."

"You'd better."

"Soon as I can stand up without my brains all churning, I'll head out of here, so's you and Amy can live in peace."

"Head out where?" Fern put a boot on the chest at the foot of my bed so she could lean on her knee.

"Well, maybe west. Everybody's going west these days."

"West, huh? Well, I been west as far as Kansas. And it ain't all they say. It's either cold or hot or windswept so heavy there's dust in everything you can name and in some of the things you shouldn't."

"I'd just like to see what it's like, out west."

"You told me the night I fished you up from the snow that you was headed for Ti."

"That's right."

"Well, your arse end is plunk dab in the middle of it. So now you're here, best you joy it some. You got folks here?"

"Maybe."

"I don't guess there's a soul in town that I don't know by name, and them me. So who is it?"

"Sabbathday."

"You kin to John?" Fern half straighted herself up and looked at me square.

"Sure am. He's a cousin or something. But I

73

haven't seen John since we used to go to school together. Ain't seen him for over a year."

Fern busted out laughing.

"So you and John Sabbathday were schoolboys together. Tit, that's remarkable. On account that John Sabbathday's been dead for about six years, and he was the yonder side of sixty. If the two of you was in school together, then I'd say old John was a might slow with his lessons."

"I guess I'm mixed up."

"Guess you are."

"Maybe it was his son I knew."

"More like a grandson if'n you ask me."

"Yeah, that was it. His son's son."

"John Sabbathday didn't have no son. All he had was one girl. A daughter. But if she got wedded and bedded, *your* name wouldn't be Sabbathday."

"No. My name's Smith."

"So you keep saying. What was your ma's name?"

"Mrs. Smith."

"Her first name?"

"Oh, her first name."

"Most folks have one," said Fern.

"Her first name was . . . Molly."

Fern took the tray off my lap and set it on the stand next to a white pitcher and washbowl. Then she come and sat on the edge of my bed. I could

74

tell that Fern was in no mood for any more stories, and that she wanted the straight of it.

"Now then," she said, "Mr. Tit Smith, there's a passel of things I want to know about you. Here you are in Ticonderoga, and you're a long ways from home if home is Cornwall. Is it?"

"Yes'm. Reckon you could say that."

"Young man, right now you happen to be in my care. Seeing I'm a doctor, I want to patch you up good and proper."

"Thanks, Fern. I mean it."

"I ain't through. You are also living under my roof and eating at my table, so I feel we make a bit more than just a doctor and patient. Agree?"

"Yes'm, I sure do."

"Then open up. All I know is you say you're Tit Smith from Cornwall, Vermont. You got yourself gunshot, and now you ask of John Sabbathday. You tell me your ma is Molly Smith, and I don't swallow one letter of it. Who shot you?"

"I don't know. It was dark of night."

"Was it man or woman?"

"I don't know that. There was a dance in Cornwall that night and somebody shot me."

"You that bad a dancer? Serious now, where's your ma and pa, the famous Mr. and Mrs. Smith that I hear so much about?"

"My mother is dead. She was shot that night and killed. Honest, Fern."

75

"I believe you."

"The reason I come to Ti is to look up my pa."

"What's his name?"

"I don't know."

"It's like that, is it?" Fern took hold of my hand and held it in hers. "No pa at all?"

"I don't know who my pa is, Fern. My mother never told me anything about him. I don't even know if his name is Sabbathday. That was my mother's. Her name was Millicent Sabbathday."

Fern sighed. "So you're Millie's boy."

"That's me. Millie's boy."

"Figured as much when you said Molly."

"That was a lie. I'm sorry, Fern."

"It weren't a bad lie, Tit. Some lies get told to hurt folks. Guess I'd be right sorry if either you or Amy told me a hurting lie."

"I wouldn't hurt you or Amy. You know that, Fern."

"I know. Now tell me more about why you come to Ti. I had you pegged for a runaway. Guess you ain't."

Sitting up in that clean white bed, with two plump pillows behind my backbone and looking up into the kindly moon-face of Fern Bodeen, I was just about to tell another lie. Then I decided not to.

"Yes, I am. I run off when the sheriff in Cornwall was writing out papers to pack me off to the County Farm. I didn't want to go there."

"What you wanted was to look for your pa?"

"That's why I started off in the middle of the night, even with a gunshot belly. All I planned to do was make Shoreham by sunup, so to beg breakfast from Sam Callum."

"You figure the sheriff would come after you?"

"No."

"No? I sure would have. It's his job, boy."

"I wrote him a note, to say that I was on my way to Ti to turn up my pa."

"Maybe you'll find him sooner than you think."

"Why'd you say that, Fern?"

"Had my reasons."

"You know something, Fern?"

"What makes you think I know anything? A fat old gal like me."

"You do. And you're telling a lie about it, Fern. You're telling a lie when you know and don't tell."

Fern threw a hand over and mussed up my hair, sort of the way Gus Tobin would do when he was in a mood to like somebody.

"You sure do got red hair, Tit Smith."

"What about it?"

"Well, it sort of reminds me of a gentleman I know who's got hair as orange and carroty as yourn."

"Tell me, Fern. Tell me!" I reached up and pushed her hand off my head.

"Easy, son. You'll open up that gun wound again. Let it mend, and let your own self mend along with it or you'll come apart in more ways than one. I know there's a hurt in you that's deeper than any old ball of lead could bury. It ain't easy to grow up and not know your pa. But remember this, Tit. A lot of your growing up is back of you. It's over and done with. Ever start to read a book?"

"Sure. Lots of times."

"Well, that's what it's like right now. When I found you that night on the Shoreham road, that was page one."

"But I got to find my pa, Fern. I honestly got to. Who's the man with red hair?"

"He don't live in Ti. And you better pull in your ribbons a bit. You're going to find a lot more in this big old world than just a pa. Your pa ain't as important as you are. Besides, there's no proof the gentleman *is* your pa. Folks who do heavy courting seldom write it all down. Be fools if they did. To back up what's no more in my head than just a guess, there ain't one lick of fact. So you can't live your life like you're in a boil of mustard."

"I just want to find my pa, that's all."

"Maybe you're trying to fly the wrong way."

"What do you mean, Fern?"

"Maybe you shouldn't try to fly from one

busted nest into another. Because when a young bird leaves the nest, he leaves it permanent. The only nest he has after that is the one he helps build for the next clutch of eggs. How old are you, Tit?"

"Sixteen. Almost seventeen."

"Too old to crawl backward."

"Backward?"

"Yes, too old to crawl back into an eggshell. When the shell is broke, it's broke for keeps. Nobody ever tell you about all the king's horses and all the king's men?"

"Couldn't put Humpty Dumpty together again."

"Right. And what I'm trying my level best to do for you, son, is to put *you* back together again, body and spirit."

I closed my eyes. All of a sudden, I felt real tired, like I could sleep for a hundred years. Under my chin, I felt Fern's hand tug the covers up snug.

"Good night, Fern. Thank you for putting me back together again. I guess I'll find out what I aim to—in time."

"In time," said Fern. "Ever see a rosebud?"

"Yes."

"You'll never force it open. Can't rip a rosebud into a rose. It's like a life, Tit. It just has to blossom in its own time, and unto its own season."

Fern picked up the tray and went out, closing the door quiet as she could. There sure was a lot of

the sweet and gentle in Doc Bodeen. All her cuss
words was just a husk. Inside, Fern was whole
wheat.

But there's something about my mother that
Fern didn't take to. I had a hunch there weren't no
love lost between Millie Sabbathday and Fern
Bodeen.

12

"Tit?"

My room was dark. But somebody was whispering my name.

"Tit!"

"Yeah?"

"It's me. Amy."

"Oh. I was sleeping. Thought it was your aunt."

"Aunt Fern's asleep. I can hear her snoring from way downstairs in the kitchen."

"Why were you down in the kitchen?"

"Couldn't sleep. So I went down to the cellar for an apple. You like Baldwins?"

"Sure do. Next to Jonathans, I guess Baldwins are about the best eating apple there is. Can I have a bite?"

"Of course. I cut it in half so we could share it."

My half of the Baldwin was cold and crisp. It

was so quiet in my room, I could hear the pockets of air pop open as I chewed up all the goodness. Even the apple skin was ripe and sweet as honey. It was hard put to tell which made me happier: eating that Baldwin apple, or knowing that Amy was here with me in the dark of night. We talked in whispers.

"Boy, that tasted fine."

"Almost as good as a Jonathan?" said Amy.

"Better."

"Aren't you going to say thank you?"

"Thanks, Amy."

"You're welcome."

"I sure do hope your aunt doesn't hear us whispering in the dark like this. If she opened that door right now, I'd like to die."

"She won't."

"How do you know?"

Amy giggled. "An apple keeps the doctor away."

I burst out laughing, and Amy stuffed a pillow over my face. Even when I put my head under the quilts, I could still hear myself laugh.

"Be quiet, Tit—you're shaking the whole bed." I could tell the way Amy said it she was laughing too.

"That's an apple a *day*," I whispered back. "It never said about an apple a night."

Amy giggled again, and now it was my turn to

put the other pillow over her face. But she turned away and wouldn't let me do it. Meanwhile she was trying to smother me with the pillow that she'd grabbed up first. Now that we each had a pillow, it would of been a two-bit shame not to have a buffet. So I hauled off and socked her a good one. Not really hard enough to hurt. But it took her by surprise when the pillow hit her stomach. It whapped some wind out of her. I heard her grunt.

"Oh," she said, "so that's the game."

A pillow hit me smack on the nose, and I didn't even see it coming. Amy must have reared back and put all she had on it. It sure got my attention. And just as I turned to see where it come from, the pillow got me back of the head. That did it. No girl was going to beat me in a pillow fight. Standing up in the middle of the big bed, I swung my pillow around me in a wide circle. It must have hit its mark, because it sure felt like a good solid hit. Hard enough to take Amy's head off. That was when I stopped swinging my pillow, which was a mistake. I never knew that girls could see in the dark, but Amy sure could. Her next blow knocked me clear off the bed and onto the floor.

Before I could get up, she hit me again. It was no use to get my own pillow into the action, as Amy was standing on it. That was when I figured to yank her off her feet with one big tug. So I yanked! There was a loud rip which left my hand holding half a pillow. Something tickled my nose and it was no use. I let out one corker of a sneeze, so hard it hurt my gut where Gus pulled the lead.

"Quiet," said Amy. "Something ripped, and it better not be my good muslin nightie or Aunt Fern will skin me sideways. Hey! Something's in my mouth."

"What is it?"

"A feather."

"That's funny," I said. "There's a feather in *my* mouth, too."

"There's feathers on the floor," said Amy, "and here's a whole pile."

"Here's more," I said. "Maybe we busted one of your Aunt Fern's pillows."

"Maybe, heck. *You* busted it. All I did was stand on the fool thing. You yanked it."

"Well, I wouldn't of if you'd had the common sense to keep your big dumb feet off it. It wasn't *your* pillow."

"I s'pose it's *yours*," whispered Amy, "and besides, I don't have big dumb feet!"

"Amy, we'll both have dumb heads unless we get the feathers back into this old pillow. How many you guess come out?"

"Not many. Just a thousand or so."

"We'll never get 'em back."

"We *have* to get them back, every single one. Come on, Tit. I'll hold the pillow case open and you stuff."

Amy held and I stuffed.

"Tit, you sure you found all the feathers? This pillow case doesn't seem to be gaining much weight."

"It's hard to see in the dark. I can just about see you. Here's another one."

"Yow! There's a feather inside my nightie, like to tickle the devil out of me. I can't reach it."

"Want me to get it?"

"Yes. Run your hand down my backbone until I say stop. Stop. Now left a little. Too far. Come back a bit. Right there. Feel it?"

"I got it. Now I lost it. It's tiny."

"It's big enough to tickle," said Amy.

"So's a piece of dust. And you can't even *see* dust."

"Yes you can."

"How?" I said.

"When a beam of sunlight comes through a window sometimes, you can see all the little stars of dust dance in the sun. It looks real beautiful. Almost like gold."

"You mean like gold dust."

"Not exactly like gold dust. That looks more like sand."

"How do you know?"

"Aunt Fern has some gold dust. She keeps it in a little chammy pouch."

"Is it worth a lot of money?"

"No, not really. Aunt Fern says it's mostly dirt, but there's supposed to be gold in it. So I guess it's not real gold dust like they fish out of rivers in California."

"Amy? You ever thought on going to California someday?"

"No, can't rightly say I have. I guess with the railroad and all, it's not such a trip. Aunt Fern said it used to take about two years, by ox wagon. It sure would be a disheartenment to poke oxen all the way to California or Oregon or someplace out west and then not find any gold."

"You know, Amy. I don't think I'd care if I found any gold at all. I'd just like to see all the beauty."

"Like what, Tit?"

"Oh, like the California valleys, with all the orchards. And the big trees. Boy, would I cotton to see them. Back in Cornwall, there was a man who'd been all the way to California and back again. He said those big redwood trees went so tall that it was small wonder they didn't scratch the sky."

"How can you scratch a sky?"

"Don't guess you could, unless you were a giant

redwood. And maybe not even then. It was just a good way to say it. A tree to scratch the sky."

"It's like poetry."

"That's why I like it."

"I didn't think boys liked poetry."

"Some say they don't, but I do. Honest, Amy. I like poetry a lot."

"So do I. Aunt Fern gave me a book of poems a year ago Christmas. Most of the poems were written by British poets."

"That's funny," I said. "You always think of the British as soldiers. You know, in red uniforms with swords and horses and cannon and stuff like that. I don't guess I ever figured they'd stop a war long enough to write verse."

"Tit, I was reading a poem once, about a war. Poetry tells about war better than just plain words."

"How come."

"Well, a poem has sort of a—a time to it. You know, like you keep time at a square dance the way you tap your foot to the music. There's music in war, music loud as thunder and drums. And a poem is sort of like the sound of marching men."

"I like to hear you talk, Amy."

"Thank you, Tit. That was a neighborly thing to say."

"I never knowed anybody who talks like you."

"What makes me so all-fired different?"

"Amy, you talk about the inside of things. Most folks just say what they see. But you can talk about stuff that you don't see, and you can make me see it too. You know what, Amy?"

"No, what?"

"I bet you could write a poem about a war, even though you didn't go."

"No, Tit. Not me. I'm not a poet."

"How do you know?"

"I tried to write a poem once."

"Let me see it, Amy."

"It was so gosh-awful, I threw it out."

"What was it about?"

"It was about Aunt Fern."

"She'd be good to write a poem about, 'cause she's sort of like a war."

"My poem was about the Fern Bodeen that folks don't see. Like you said, Tit. You can't tell what's inside my aunt by what she says. But if you watch her right close, the way she bends over and picks up a hoof on one of her mules, you can see inside her. She wouldn't be partial to it, but I can see right through my Aunt Fern. I know things about her she'd never guess I know. I'd love her no matter how much of her I saw. She's just Fern, and she's made for loving."

I wanted to say "so are you" to Amy, but the words got stuck in my craw like a turkey bone. So all I said was: "Here's another feather."

"Tit, I'm sure glad there's no light on in this room."

"How come?"

"You know what I bet it looks like?"

"You tell me."

"I bet it looks like a place where somebody killed a chicken."

I started to giggle again, and Amy put her hand over my mouth. That's when I played it possum, and I pretended to giggle more and more—so she'd keep her soft warm hand on my mouth.

I was pretending to kiss her face.

13

Breakfast the next morning was my first out-a-bed meal since I come to Ticonderoga.

"Flapjacks," said Fern, stacking the golden circles on my plate. "Butter 'em now, while they're hot."

"Please pass the maple syrup," said Amy.

Passing the syrup crock, I done my trustful best not to look at Amy. She was opening up her red-check napkin, just as I hoped she would, when the feather fell out and onto her plate. I'd hid it in her napkin when she was still upstairs getting dressed for school, and while Fern was beating the batter. Soon as Amy saw the feather she busted out a giggle. Fern was taking her spot at the head of the table, and she looked first at Amy and then at me.

"It's a feather," said Amy.

"Well, I'll be tickled," said Fern.

That's when I busted out laughing.

"It fell out of Amy's napkin," I said between snorts.

"Sure it did," said Fern. "Feathers grow on napkins every day." She picked it up and looked at it. "Seems to me I seen this here feather before. Looks familiar. And I think I know where I seen it."

"Where?" I said.

"In one of your pillows," said Fern. "I wonder how it got out. Yessir, I'd know this here goose feather anywhere. It's number eighty-eight."

"Number eighty-eight?" said Amy.

"Sure," said Fern, setting down her white mug of hot coffee. "When you stuff a pillow with feathers, you can't just march 'em in helter-skelter. They got to go in order. Look here, Tit. See the color of that feather."

"It's white," I said.

"Yes, and that's why it's a even number. Like eighty-eight. Gray and brown feathers are odd. Straight feathers go in first 'cause you want them in the center for a core. Notice the curl to this feather. Yup, I'd bet my long-and-strongs that this here feather is number eighty-eight."

"That's right, Tit," said Amy. "I helped Aunt Fern stuff those pillows and that's where it came from."

"You mean during our pillow fight?" I said.

Amy said nothing. She just closed her eyes. Fern's fingers started to drum on the table, sort of sounding like a horse going over a wood bridge at a slow canter. A very long bridge.

"Who's room?" said Fern at last.

"Mine," I said.

Amy didn't say boo. She just sat there and chewed away at flapjacks and barrow bacon, without a bother to look at her aunt.

"You'll be late for school," said Fern.

"If I am, then it'll be the only time. I'm often the first one there."

"Good," said Fern. "And wear a muffler. The mercury says it's above zero, but not so you'd notice."

Amy put on her coat and boots; and with a scarf over her head, she went out the kitchen door. I helped Fern clear the kitchen table and do up the breakfast crockery, including the big black griddle that Fern poured out jacks on. Then I started back upstairs to my room, to see if I could spot a stray feather before Fern did. And to rest my gut.

"Whoa," said Fern.

"I was just going upstairs to make up my bed."

"The bed can wait. Take a seat while I have another coffee."

"Sure."

"I already spoke to Mr. Delano about you, Tit."

"Who's he?"

"The man who owns the Ti Pulp. That's short for the Ticonderoga Pulp & Paper Company. I asked him to take you on; and what's more, I vouched for you personal. You're not a big lad, so meeting Clayton Delano won't help none—seeing as we're going to start your paper-making career logging with Ostrander and his crew. Soon as you mend, we'll ship you north."

"Is Ostrander some sort of boss?"

"That's right. He'll be your boss. And I can tell you ahead of time, he won't be an easy boss to sweat for. You'll earn your pay with Ostrander, 'cause there ain't a manjack who works for him who's got a cool saw."

"I don't mind, Fern. I like to work. And if you vouch for me with Mr. Delano, I won't let you down."

"Thanks, Tit. I was hopin' you'd say that. I weren't trying to water your fire. Just explaining what it'll be like hauling spruce for Ostrander."

"He sounds like a strong man."

"Strong, yes. But not big. Hardly bigger than you, Ostrander is. And surely not bigger than me." Fern laughed.

"What's he like?"

"Tough, quiet sometimes. Hardly says much. And he's got to be one of the most lonely critters north of hell."

"I guess where he works it's a lonely life."

"He weren't always lonely," said Fern. "A few years back, Ostrander had a wife and daughter. His wife's name was Mary; and to hear Ostrander talk, she was about the best wife since Kingdom Come. I guess Mary was the only wife Ostrander ever wanted. I heard her play the pump organ more than one time. She could really make that old box sing. Ostrander went all the way to Glens Falls and back to buy that organ. He had the stops special-made of real rosewood with ivory centers. Mother-of-pearl back of the keys. He hauled it all the way to Ironville for her. Just him and his team."

"How far is that?"

"Must be nigh to sixty mile, one way. Took him four days to do it."

"Your friend Mr. Ostrander must like organ music a whole lot."

"Not no more, Tit. Him and Mary had a daughter, Nell. Mary taught little Nell to play the organ, a few simple songs. Nell was still too small for her feet to reach the pedals. But she could play things like 'Jesus, Lover of My Soul' with one finger. I heard her do it."

"How'd she reach the pedals?"

"Ostrander himself. He sat on the organ bench and put his boots to the squares and worked those pedals, holding Nell on his lap so she could play. It really made Mary and me laugh to see it.

Ostrander took a real rib about it, too. Some of his old woodhooks got wind of it and when some bulletin got writ up at the Moravian church, they doctored it up to read 'Organist: G. W. Ostrander.' "

"He must of got a laugh out of it."

"He sure did. But I don't guess, boy, that Ostrander's laughed since. Not one time."

"What happened?"

"Ostrander come home one night late. Found both Mary and Nell dead on the parlor floor."

"What from?"

"Redhide Indians. There was a Indian or two worked on the log gang. One's name was Numbers, and he had a son called Tahawus. Good workers when they was sober. So Ostrander wouldn't let 'em near hootch. Drunks and heavy timber don't mix. Not on the job, and not near no sawmill. That's where Numbers worked; with his son, Tahawus."

"Tahawus. That sure is an odd one."

"It means Thomas, I guess. He got fired by Ostrander for reasons of drink, to save *his* life as well as the arms and hands of men who worked the saw along beside him."

"What happened then?"

"Thomas was sore for getting laid off. He come at Ostrander with a pike pole. Caught him in the shoulder and spun him around. Ostrander got the

95

better of him that day, but he made a big mistake."

"Like what?"

"Ostrander should of killed him. A day later, Thomas and four other drunk redhides took revenge on Mary and Nell. I was up in Ironville that night and I saw it all, Tit. And I hope no man on this earth comes home to what Ostrander come home to that night. Blood all over, like you'd throwed a bucket of red paint."

"God!"

"Ostrander didn't go to bed for three nights. He just walked up and down the quiet road, thinking up revenge."

"Did he know who done it?"

"He knew. Thomas and them other four had been in town, liquored up and mean mouth. Talking big talk."

"What did Ostrander do about it?"

"Nothing, for a week or so. Nell had a pet dog, a half-growed pup named Turk. Just a floppy old pup with big clumsy paws. Turk was to be a watchdog. Not yet big enough to bite, but plenty big to bark. But the night Mary and Nell got slain, Turk had run off on a rabbit track. That's when Ostrander started schooling Turk to be an Indian dog."

"An Indian dog?"

"Yeah, and when Thomas come back to town, which weren't too smart, Ostrander let Turk rip that young redhide from stem to sternum. That made one, with four more to go. Any four, as far as Ostrander feels. Long as they belong to the Saint Francis tribe."

"Is that what Numbers and Thomas and the others all are?"

"That's what they be. Saint Francis. The meanest bunch of redhides east of Kansas. And I guess that Ostrander figures he'll be that much meaner."

"Is he really rotten mean?" I said.

"He's an animal in pants. A hurt animal. Ever see an animal with a leg in a trap?"

"No."

"Well, I have. A critter with a leg in iron will bite anything, just to hurt back. It'll even bite its own leg, because its own hurt drives it mad. Ostrander's that kind of an animal."

Maybe Fern was telling me all this 'cause Ostrander was going to be my boss. That could of been it. Fern had a reason for things she said and did. But it all run a bit deeper than that. It was more than just business. Fern knew more than her prayers.

"Fern, how come you told me all this stuff about Ostrander?"

"Because about seventeen year ago, he used to come to Ti an court a certain gal."

"Who?"

"Millicent Sabbathday."

14

"There's been an accident," said Fern, as she come banging right through the front door. "Some of Ostrander's men."

Ten days went by, and I was living with Fern and Amy. Just until I got glued back together. They had a small house in Ticonderoga, just the two of them. It seemed that Fern Bodeen was all the kin that Amy Hallow had.

Fern's house in Ti weren't fancy furnished, but it was cozy and warm to take board in. What there was was right up to snuff. It even had an iron deer on the lawn. As it turned out, Fern was the "mill doctor." The town had another doctor and that was Doctor Turner. But whoever worked in the paper mill and needed medical assistance got doctoring by Doc Bodeen, for free.

"Ironville," said Fern, when Amy asked her

where the accident happened. "Ten miles away and it's all uphill. And the road ain't as good as a cowpath."

"Who was hurt?"

"Ray Cox, and two more on Ostrander's crew. I got the call from Mr. Delano to head up Ironville way and pronto. You able to travel, Tit?"

"Yes'm."

"Good," said Fern. Now's the time to do it. It's a rough ten-mile trip, so get packing and pack to stay for all winter. Don't take nothing that ain't wool. Did them clothes Mrs. Harmon sent over fit?"

"Yes'm, they fit real good. Except that the underwear's a bit scratchy."

"It won't be scratchy, boy, once we git north country. That's why I wear my long-songs, winter and summer."

"You wear 'em in summer, too?"

"Bet I do. Every spring, I just take out the trapdoor and put in a screen. Haw, haw, haw!"

Fern almost died over her own joke. I looked to see if Amy'd blush. No sign. She was no doubt used to her Aunt Fern's leg-slappers. I also took note that while her aunt and I were swapping words, Amy was busy taking medicines from a cabinet and filling up one of Fern's several black doctoring bags. She selected each tool careful, thinking on it real well before it went into the bag.

"Don't stand there, Tit. Move! Pack your duds and then roll up three blankets each. That's nine, to my way of counting."

"Nine?" Amy said. "You—you mean *I'm* coming, too?"

"You surely are, girl. That is if'n you can bear to·miss a day of school. Besides, it almost Christmas recess anyhow."

Rolling up the quilts, I was happy as a mated clam. Amy was coming along! This sure was a surprise to me. I knew that I was well enough to go to work. And also that I just couldn't camp at Fern's house much longer. The idea of leaving Amy in Ticonderoga and going to a log site in Ironville for the winter was lonely to think on.

"What else did Mr. Delano say about the accident, Aunt Fern?"

"Bad," said Fern. "Ray Cox is tore up so bad they dassn't move him. We'll have a guide to Ironville, as Mr. Delano doesn't want me to head out alone with just the mules for company. Amy, if'n Clayt Delano knew I was taking you up north, it'd attack his heart."

"Who's our guide, Aunt Fern?"

"Sabatis. Mr. Delano is sending for him, but I don't guess he'll be here much before morning, old as he is. Delano couldn't find no one else. Let's see now, what'd I say at noon that we'd heat up for supper?"

"Mutton," said Amy.

Fern Bodeen wasn't much on the pride of owning worldly goods. But other than Amy and her two mules, the one "calefaction" (as she put it) in Fern's life was her stove. It was no small item, but I figured that old Fern never went nowhere without it—and a good can of graphite to black it. According to Amy, the stove was always in her kitchen at home, and always in her wagon when she up and outed. It sure was some stove, and Fern loved it dearly. Even had a name for it: Mantrap.

"Love don't linger," Fern said, "like cookin' do."

And the fact that her stove was called Mantrap said it all about Fern's personal brand of hunger. Mantrap could of stewed a moose. It was an 1893 Acme American, and it took four men (as I saw next morning) to put to a wagon. Mantrap balanced at 420 pounds. Six lids, over ten square feet of cooking top, and enough oven to brown three pies and swell up six loaves of bread. Mantrap sure was a modern contraption. It even had shake-grates to free the ashes, so as they could fall into a pullout ash box. Plus a double warming oven up top to keep the biscuits hot. Just about everything that Mantrap was made up of was lettered on its big black side. The whole business was stamped right into the iron, and framed all around by swirls and fancy vines. You'd swear it come right from Paris,

France. And practical? Fern said that Mantrap could slow-cook a twenty-five-pound turkey, and to take ten hours was the only way to do it.

"Supplies," said Fern. "Here's a list, boy. Go get 'em laded and loaded and charged to the Ti Pulp. Now git."

It was late afternoon in Ticonderoga. The western sun was shining pink on Exchange Street which was the town's main street of business. And it sure was a bustle of a place. Ti was the biggest settlement I'd ever been to. It was over eight hundred families. And on Exchange Street alone, I must of added up a good twenty-five stores. All this besides the Ti Pulp and a graphite works. (They called graphite "black lead.")

I walked along Exchange Street, taking note of all the business establishments. Harvey's Tannery, a forge, the Joseph Weed Lumber Company, sleigh makers by the names of Joshua Halcomb and J. B. Ramsey, a cooper, an office for the Delaware & Hudson Canal Company, drygoods, tailor, hardware, tinsmith, blacksmith, harness maker, dentist, bootery, barber shop, gristmill, livery stable, Ledger's Inn, the Burleigh House Hotel, and Ives Opera House. Not to forget three saloons. Two were nameless, but the third owner displayed his name proud and prominent. The frosty glass window said "Tim Blake's."

Adkins & Scott was where I was headed; but

102

there was so many points of interest along the way, it was amazing I got there. Adkins & Scott was a supplier for Ti Pulp, and they sold it all. One foot inside the door told me that if Adkins & Scott didn't trade it, it weren't worth the purchase.

I figured on not getting as much as a how-do in that store. But when I told a clerk what I had (an order charged to the Ti Pulp), it was not other than Mr. Arthur Adkins himself who come to fill it. Fatback, beans, bacon, and five kinds of apples: Jilliflower, Maiden's Blush, Cortland, Russet, and Spetzenberg. We got salted salmon, a sack of potatoes, two loaves of fresh bread and a firkin of butter, a leg of Merino mutton, a side of beef, a small box of Fern's special candy, salt, sugar, flour, a churn of lard, one wheel of rat cheese, a fine-cut plug of tobacco, and a dozen bars of *soap*. Fern Bodeen sure was one loyal marcher in the ranks of cleanliness.

"Now then," said Mr. Adkins, squinting at my list, "if I can make out Doc Bodeen's fine hand, you'll want feedstore supplies, too. They're all in the back."

Added to the pile was a wad of excelsior, a bolt of tar paper, a corked-and-sealed glass bottle of citronella, putty, rope, a bar of saddle soap, creosote, a salt block, linseed and cottonseed oil, a hunk of resin, turpentine, Javelle water (the aromatic variety), a sack of oats, and some sunflower seeds.

103

Getting the turpentine was a problem, until Mr. Adkins showed me how to tap the turp barrel and crank out a measure. It sure had a smell to it, enough to float a horseshoe.

"Say," said Mr. Adkins, who I was sure knew that Fern didn't cotton to traveling light, "how about some ice-cream salt? Can't make ice cream without salt."

"Fine with me," I said.

On the way back to Fern's house, I passed by the home of the Reverend Harmon and his wife. But then I went back and knocked at their door. Just to say a thank you for the clothes they sent over for me to wear. If'n it wasn't for the Harmon family, my arse end would of been naked in the snow—seeing as Fern put a match to everything I wore except coat and boots. I told Fern about it, about stopping to give thanks to the Harmons.

"Good boy, Tit," said Fern. "The only prayer that counts is gratefulness."

15

"The worst smell in town," Gus Tobin had once said to me, "is the stench of a redhide Indian that's been dead for three days."

True or no, the first whiff I got of our guide that morning would of gagged a maggot. He was standing in the kitchen, about as close to Mantrap as he could get without cooking himself. There was mocs on his feet, and his lower legs were wrapped in leggins. His pants and shirt was deerskin, so old they was almost black—and so stiff with grease they looked about to crack and fall off.

Around his shoulders was several blankets; and you'd be hard put to tell just how many, as they was all wadded and twisted tight about him. His hair was long, in a single braid, and entire white. But a dirty white. On his head was a wide-brim felt hat with a lone black crow's feather stuck in the rawhide hat band. Straight up.

"This here is Sabatis," said Fern, who was breaking brown eggs into a black spider. "His people can't say Saint John the Baptist. The French told 'em it was Sah Batiste, so you can see how it got from there to Sabatis. He's the one Delano sent to point us all toward Ironville."

"Ad-iron-dack," was what Sabatis grunted.

"Howdy," I said in return.

Sabatis did not speak again. He just gave a nod of his head, turned his back to me, and fanned his old leathery hands over the stove. I wasn't the only one who'd took a sad scent of him. Fern, I noted, had the door open—even though it was dark and December.

"Ad-iron-dack," said Fern, pouring eggs on a hot plate. "I don't know much of the Abenakee tongue, but I figured what *that* means."

"I thought it was hello," I said.

"Naw," said Fern. "Adirondack means *where iron is*. Just like you or me or Amy would call it Ironville. Our old friend Sabatis calls it Adirondack. I kind of like it. Then again, somebody else said it meant *bark-eater*."

"Where is Ironville?" I said.

"West of Crown Point, the way I got it smelled out," said Fern.

"I wondered what that smell was," said Amy, as

106

she entered the kitchen. "Now I know. It's the fragrance of West Crown Point."

With her free hand, Fern stuffed a biscuit roll into Amy's mouth. As she did it, she didn't say a word nor did she have to. I reckoned that Fern didn't cotton to having Sabatis in her kitchen any more than I did, Fern being so high on washing and all. But neither was anybody (not even Amy) going to say words to hurt folks. Not under Fern's roof. If that old redhide got wind of what was said, he never let on. He just stood alongside the stove, letting Mantrap warm him, lifting up one foot and then the other, and trying to thaw the stiff out of his skinny old toes.

Besides eggs, Fern served up sidepork, slices of fried potato, hot coffee, and biscuits with honey. All the time we sat at the lammis table in the kitchen, Sabatis stood near the stove. My back was to him. Yet I could feel those black eyes of his. I could feel 'em on the back of my neck, crawling up into my hair. It was as if two lice was on your head that you weren't allowed to scratch. It was like he had seen me before. It gave my shoulders a shudder just before he spoke.

"Ostrander."

It sounded like Sabatis had spat out the name. And as I turned, the old guide was pointing at me.

"That's right," said Fern. "We're all going to

Adirondack to see Ostrander." She said it too fast, like she was trying to shut Sabatis up.

Sabatis said no more. From somewhere inside the folds of blankets he pulled out a half-eaten ear of sweet corn. I expected to see him gnaw on it the way a starved rat would. But instead he broke off each kernel one by each, placed each one atop the stove, crushed it with the handle of a skinning knife, and tossed the pulp into his mouth. It was then I knew why. Our guide Sabatis was missing something. Teeth.

Some men came (sent by Mr. Delano) and we loaded up Fern's wagon. As we had to let Mantrap cool after heating up breakfast, the old black Acme American cookstove was the last to get loaded. And it was still warm enough to cozy the wagon. No wonder Fern's "calefaction" was also her traveling furnace. That done, the four of us left the town of Ticonderoga and headed west, up the hill of Exchange Street and through the gray of morning.

It was uphill all the way. At least all the way up Chilson Hill. Amy was the lightest in weight, so she sat the seat and held the ribbons while Sabatis walked in front. Fern and I trailed behind the wagon.

"Fern?" I said.

"I'm listening. Don't ask me talk while I'm hoofing up this cussed hill."

"Sabatis don't like me."

"Nonsense."

"Honest, Fern. It's just something I feel, and it hits me extra hard when my back is turned."

"You imagine too much. You're like Amy."

"Maybe so, Fern. But I'm sure about one thing. Sabatis knows something about me, and what he knows he don't like."

"He's just sore," said Fern.

"At me?"

"Naw. He's mad with Delano for sending him to Ironville. And I'm mad with Delano for the same blessed reason, for giving us a guide that's got a grudge against the place we're all headed for."

"Why are you stopping?"

"I got to either talk or climb. So let's whoa a minute. Just to be sure Sabatis don't ear it."

"You don't trust Sabatis?" I asked.

"Yeah, I trust that red devil. I trust him as far as I can throw Mantrap."

"Then maybe we ought to catch up, and not let Amy and Sabatis get too far ahead. So if he tries anything funny, we can put a no to it."

"No danger," said Fern. "We ain't even uphill to Gooseneck yet. If old Sabatis plots treachery, it'll be close to Ironville. That's where he'll be thinking on getting near to Ostrander. And that's when I'll load my old Monkey-Ward shotgun and tote it under my arm."

"What's Sabatis sore at, if it ain't me?"

"It ain't you," said Fern. "But you're right, Tit. Sabatis is sore at Ostrander, because of what happened to his grandson."

"His grandson?"

"Yeah," said Fern. "His grandson Tahawus."

"Was that the Indian they called Thomas?"

"The very one, and he was the son of Numbers who was son of Sabatis. Get the picture?"

"I get it. Sabatis don't cotton to go near Ironville. But do you think Ostrander would kill that old man?"

"Before you could spit," said Fern. "Right now, that old Indian is thinking about just what we're talking about. He knows we all been friends to the Ostranders."

"Let's catch up, Fern."

"You run on ahead," said Fern. "Tell my niece to rest them mules with a rock behind the wheel until I get there. I ain't of a mind to trot up Chilson Hill to please a man or the Devil."

We stopped to water the mules, at a place called Gooseneck Pond, on a road that was covered with snow hardpacked from sleighs and wagons. It hadn't snowed in near a week, and a passel of folks lived up Chilson way. We saw farm after farm all the way to Gooseneck.

The "girls"—Jack and Jenny—had sweated up some from the uphill of it; and while the mules took their water, Fern and me wiped 'em dry with a pair of blankets that Fern tucked under the wagon bench for just such a purpose. Doc Bodeen sure was a fine lady when it come to tending and mending.

From the watering spot at Gooseneck Pond, we continued west toward Eagle Lake. The path was flat out now, and Fern sat the seat alongside of her niece. Sabatis and I walked in front of the mules. The sun was up, and it gave both of us a long blue shadow as it hit our backs. Like I said, I walked with Sabatis—but not really at his side. No word passed betwixt that old redhide and me. Not even one. The only sound was the breathing of the mules behind us, and once in while a singing duet from Fern and Amy. They did right good on "Oh, the Moon Shines Tonight on Pretty Red-Wing."

It was all so piney and peaceable that I got to thinking about myself. "No father, no mother, no known kin," as Gus Tobin had put in his report. Then there was the crumpled-up petition, the one for a pauper to be a county charge. And the rubbed-out name of Millicent Sabbathday, a lady who'd come to Cornwall and called herself Millie Smith. And me Tit.

As I walked along, I could feel the lead in my pocket. It was the same hunk of lead that Gus Tobin picked out of me. And here I be, headed west with a trio of strangers, instead of staying in

111

Ti to learn some about Millie's past. Now I was headed to a place called Ironville to work for Ostrander. Maybe Sabatis already knew something. Possible he knew more, like Fern, and wasn't about to tell me any more than Gus did. If the answer was back in the town of Ti, I was sure pointed wrong to uncover it. But there wasn't any turning around now. A boy of sixteen had to make his own path and earn his own salt. For a while my home would be Ironville. My old U.S. Army kitsack was back in Fern Bodeen's wagon; packed with all my earthly goods, including what I really prized now more than anything else. The picture of my mother in the oval amber frame.

Last night, before going to sleep, I'd taken out that picture of Millie and looked at it. Millicent Sabbathday had been a fair young lass. But she wasn't weak and frail. Her face had—I finally thought of the word—character. And the more I held that picture in my hands, the prouder I got that Tit Smith was her son. I returned the oval amber picture to where I safe-keeped it, wrapped inside my extra shirt—the blue one. I always kept the picture right close to my Bible. It sure seemed a fit and proper place to store a picture of somebody's mother. I hoped that nobody would find it, deep as it was inside my U.S. Army kitsack.

I was thinking about the log crew, and wondering just how hard it would be to work for Ostrander.

It was plain that Sabatis had no use for him. Other than that one talk we had, I couldn't get as much as a peep out of Fern. And if Fern mentioned his name, Amy made a face. It was just enough of a sour look to tell me that she didn't much cotton to the man. I never did ask why. I just reckoned that up in Ironville, Ostrander was the boss and a boss ain't always popular. But everybody said that Ostrander's timber crew was the place to start, if you had a notion to study the trade of paper-making.

We forded Eagle Lake and turned north onto a road that Fern said was called "Stony Lonesome." It weren't much more than a log road, and the logs had sunk deep into the ice of winter and mud of spring. In spots, the road was bare and windswept, a road that was true to its name. It was stony, and it sure was lonesome. We didn't even stop for a noon meal, but just keeped on moving north to-ward Ironville. We had to push the wagon and break snow, on account of some of the drifts swal-lowed the path—just like we was in woods and there was no path. But old Sabatis knew the way.

I knew we were nearing Ironville when I saw Fern push a shell into her 12-gauge Texas Ranger shotgun. It would be dark soon, and she wasn't going to let Sabatis quit on us—seeing as he might already have his pay in his pocket. So, for the last mile, Fern never took her eyes off Sabatis. If'n he'd took one step off what she figured the trail was, Fern would of unloaded that gun. The hot way. I had me a hunch that not too many souls ever crossed the path of Fern Bodeen.

Just before it got dark, we saw a sign that was cut into a big pin-oak. It was a big *O* with a *GW* inside it. Then we saw another, and then plenty more as we drawed closer to the lamp lights of Ironville. We even passed a wagon that bore the same sign, burned right to the wood. And branded onto the rumps of the oxen.

"Hey, Fern," I said, "you got any idea what GWO means?"

"Sure do," said Fern. "That, my dear boy, stands for something you'll know soon enough."

"Like what?"

"George Washington Ostrander."

16

"Hey, Jake! How's your kidneys?"

Even though it was pitch dark when we come to a halt, Fern yelled to the first soul we saw in the tiny town of Ironville as if he'd been long-lost kin.

"Doing just fine, Doc. How's yours?"

"None of your business, you old termite!"

"I aim to make it my business."

"*You'll* sooner be in a pig's ear."

Jack and Jenny stopped at a small, white-painted shack. Over the door was a long sign that said "Property of Ticonderoga Pulp & Paper Company." Before we could hardly tie up the reins, Jake appeared with three men, as if it'd all been planned.

"We'll unload for ya, Doc. Stove and all. But you better go see Ray Cox."

"How bad is he, Jake?"

"Real bad. Some say dying."

"Who said?"

"Ostrander."

"What would he know about living or dying. Got a cutter?"

"Hitched and ready, Doc. One of my sons, Ernest, will drive you to where Ray's laid up."

"Let's be about it. Amy where's my bag?"

"Right here, Aunt Fern."

"I'll be back, soon's I tend what needs tending. Ray Cox and them other two."

Jake and his pals unloaded Mantrap. Inside the shack was a spot against a far wall for the old stove to nest down, as if it'd been there many times. It had, said Amy. The men helped with a few of the heavier boxes and bales, said good night, and left. Amy started setting things up cozy inside, while I pulled the wagon to beside the shack and un-hitched "the girls." There was a divided box stall out back, complete with oats and dry straw. So be-fore I come inside, I saw fit that both mules were bedded and boarded and blanketed for night.

As I was wooling off Jenny, so she'd sleep real good after a lively rubdown, I started wondering where Sabatis was. He'd gone off, but I don't re-call just when. Sometime during the ruckus be-tween Fern and Jake and everybody talking all to once, that old redhide just up and melted into Iron-ville—without as much as a so-long. I wanted to talk to Sabatis, providing he could talk, and ask him some things I figured he knew. His owl eyes knew more than he let out. But I never got the chance. He went off like smoke. Maybe his people lived outside Ironville. I knew that Sabatis had a grandson that was killed some time ago, his throat tore open. And no wolf did it. I wanted to ask Sabatis, but he took leave. I don't guess I cared much, on account of it left me alone with Amy.

When I finally stomped inside, there she was. And being alone with her always seemed to make her prettier than regular, if that was possible. There was always so much inside me that I wanted to say to Amy and never had the chance to. But any time I was alone with her, my tonsils were dry as bone and my heart went to beating like I feared she could hear it, clear across the room. When I looked at Amy or heard her voice, singing "Whispering Hope" as she did helping me do up the supper dishes back in Ticonderoga, it was like what was passed didn't account for a whit. It didn't matter who or what I was, as far as a name. This is how I felt as I kicked the doorjamb to get the snow off my boots. The fireplace was roaring and bright. Amy had lit a lamp and the light helped thaw the cold.

"Well," said Amy, "this is Ironville."

"You been here before?"

"Yes, last summer and the summer before. Always with Aunt Fern, of course. This is my first trip to Ironville in the dead of winter. It looks a lot different at night and with all the snow. Some of the turns in the road looked brand new."

"Good thing we had Sabatis."

"Looks as though we don't have him now. As soon as we arrived, he up and left. All he had to do was hear Ostrander's name. Besides that, I think the old man had a thirst."

"And I got a hunger. What's for supper, Amy?"

"Nothing, unless you get Mantrap heated up. Usually you can find a pile of stove wood out back."

Under a lip of the back roof there was wood aplenty. Logs for the fireplace and split for the cookstove. As I lugged in the first armful, I noticed that the wood was cut to Fern's liking—and took a guess that Jake must have put an axe to it. As old Fern let go an opinion on just about everything, she let it be knowed her preference on firewood. Rock maple was to cook by, 'cause it burned hot. Softwood burned up too fast and didn't hardly leave a coal to bake on. Back in Ticonderoga, she had an axe in my hand the second day I was there. Some green wood arrived, which splits easier than when it's dry and seasoned over. According to Fern Bodeen, if you can't split it ripe you got to let it winter. Froze wood can split up easy because it's brittle.

I got a corker of a fire going in Mantrap. That old big hunk of black pig iron weren't black for long. Four of the griddles started to pink up as bright as a big round cherry, and so was the yoke in between. Being as it got too hot for anybody to handle without a potholder, I took the lifter out of its griddle navel and let it rest atop the warming oven.

"Water," said Amy as she tossed me a bucket, "is outside in a barrel. You may have to break the ice, so mind you don't break the barrel. Ironville doesn't have a cooper, and Aunt Fern brung that barrel all the way up from Ti."

"Water coming," I said.

I didn't much cotton to being bossed about by a slip of a girl like Amy. But seeing she was fixing to cook my supper, I don't guess I had a kick coming. Besides, I liked helping. I liked doing for Amy and Fern, and to watch either one of them stand at Mantrap and stir a pot was a sight to see.

Millie hardly ever cooked anything. I took a lot of my meals alone, down in the Maple House restaurant below where we lived. Lots of times I'd take up a tray to her. But most the time she was too bottle-sick to wolf it down. So it was a real treat for me to see a woman at a stove. I reckon I don't know the first thing about cooking, but I sure was a master at eating. Anybody who slept under Fern's roof just had to be proper fed.

"Amy," I said, as she sorted the big white beans before they went to boiling, "you sure ought to be some cook by the time you're a growed woman. You'll be a better cook even than Fern."

"Not me," said Amy.

"You're not fond of cookery?"

"Amy Hallow is going to be a doctor."

"You mean sort of a nurse-doctor, like Fern?"

"No, not like Aunt Fern. I mean like Doctor Turner. Don't you think I'm able?"

"Sure, but . . ."

"Then if I'm able enough to doctor, why just only cook? If you think it's so all-fired heavenly to stand at a stove all day, and at a sink all evening, then *you* cook. Me, I'm for doctoring."

"It takes a lot of schooling to be a doctor."

"Girls go to school, or don't you notice?"

"I notice."

"Another thing you can notice, now that you're so good at noticing. I am already more than a girl. I'm a woman."

"You're only sixteen."

"I am a *woman*. I bet I can even have a baby, any time I want a baby. I could have your baby, or any man's baby. I am a woman, Tit Smith. And not because I can have a baby, or cook a meal, or scrub a floor. It's because I *know* that I'm a woman and I don't have to prove it. All I want to do now is go to Middlebury College and study doctoring and practice medicine. That's what a full-bloom woman can do, and I aim to do it."

"Amy, I don't have no doubt you will. I don't doubt that you'll put stitches in a mill hand that needs sewing, and mend him up as proper as peace. Just as good as Fern."

"Better."

"Better than Fern?"

"You heard. Better. Aunt Fern didn't go to medical school, and there's a lot being discovered about medicine that my aunt wouldn't know of. We get a medical journal in the mail most every month. She hardly has time to read it."

"But you do."

"You bet I do. More than that, I intend to write a paper on one of the problems of rheumatoid arthritis."

"What's that?"

"Sciatica to you. And if that's still too fancy, call it lumbago."

"You're writing a story on lumbago?"

"A paper on rheumatoid arthritis sounds a mite more professional."

"I'd guess to write on something as fandangled as that, a person'd have to be a doctor."

"I will be a doctor. And what's more, perhaps even a surgeon. But for now, my study on arthritis is about salicylates. Why does aspirin work so well on headaches and yet waste away when it comes to arthritis? Some salicylate potency is lost somewhere in the body of the arthritic. Maybe it gets sluffed off or blocked by defective tissue. Or just plain used up."

"Amy, you're showing off."

"I guess I am, Tit. Sorry. I was bent to impress on you that I'm more than 'a girl.' "

You're a lot more than just a girl, Amy. Leastwise, you are to me."

While we were talking, I was soaking a slab of pork in some cold fresh water to work out some of the salt. Beans aren't much without pork. All the time Amy talked, I wanted to stand up and put my arms around her and kiss her (especially when she said she was a woman who could have my baby). But what girl wants to get herself hugged by a boy with a slick of pork fat all over his hands? So I just sat there with my rump on that dumb old stool, working the pork like it was all I ever hoped to do. The whole feeling of seeing Amy in that calico apron and all, cooking my supper, the whole doggone business of me just aching to kiss her would of been lost, but Amy saved it. She turned around to face me, bent down, and put her soft sweet mouth right to mine. She even closed her eyes. And just when I was getting over the shock of it . . .

"Come on," she said, "before you rinse that pork all night. It's time for supper."

17

Hot pork, beans, butter biscuits with honey, tea, and a cold apple with a cut of rat cheese for dessert. That was our supper.

After the meal, I helped clean up. And then Amy and I put a blanket on the floor in front of the fire and waited for Fern. The fire was dying down, but the shack was still cook-warm from Mantrap. It was nice to just lie there on your belly and see the flame fly around the logs, and to watch the red turn to gray.

"Tit."

"Yeah."

"Who are you?"

"Tit Smith. That's all you need to know."

"Just a boy with red hair that my Aunt Fern drags home and hopes to keep, is that what you ask me to believe?"

"I run away from home. But that's not true no more. I don't have a home, except with you and Fern."

"You don't have a mother or father?"

"Nobody."

"Where were you raised?"

"Vermont."

"I already know that. Aunt Fern left on a trip to Middlebury and home she comes with you."

"That's right. And you're not the only one who's curious. How come your aunt went cross-lake in the snow and all? Not just to see if Vermont looks like the December page on a calendar."

"Aunt Fern went to Middlebury to see the college and talk to someone she knows there."

"What about?"

"Me."

"You?"

"Aunt Fern is trying to get me accepted as a student."

"She knows you want to be a doctor?"

"She knows."

"I bet she's glad of it."

"She is. But I grant this to Aunt Fern. She never pushed me into medicine."

"How did you start wanting to learn all about doctoring and all?"

"Watching her. Lots of times I'd be home when one of the men at the Ti Pulp would be injured.

Paper mills are killers. They'd drag in some poor man that had his arm almost torn off in a paper machine, and I'd watch her sew him back together so as he could walk around whole. Fern Bodeen is no authority on medical theory. But she can patch people."

"Isn't that what doctoring's all about?"

"Sure is," said Amy. "It sure is. That and knowing what kicked 'em apart in the first place. Pull up your shirt."

"My shirt?"

"Yes, pull it up, please. I want to see your bullet hole."

"My *what?*"

"Bullet hole. The day you stepped out of that tub of hot mustard water that Aunt Fern soaked you in, I saw that purple spot on your belly, big as a penny."

"Aw, I bet your old aunt told you that I'd got myself shot up."

"Lending a hand to a doctor in a tough mill town like Ticonderoga, I have seen plenty of bullet holes, so stop being so muley and pull up your shirt."

"It's not under my shirt."

"I know. I saw where it is. It's on your little white belly. Unbuckle your belt."

"It's all healed up. Fern told me not to finger it and just let it be and scab over."

"I need more light. I'll get the lamp down close. It did scab over all right. You got a belly bump on you like a ripe plum and twice as purple. Like you got two belly buttons, and your spare one is just farther south."

"Amy, for a girl, you talk shocking."

"Do I shock you?"

"Gosh if you don't sometimes."

"Well, then you better cover your ears as well as your belly. You never did say who shot you."

"No, I never did."

"Was that why you ran away?"

"That's why. At least it's part of it."

"Who shot you?"

"Somebody."

"Somebody in Vermont?"

"Yes."

"Which town?"

"Cornwall."

"That's funny. Aunt Fern knows folks in Cornwall."

"You wouldn't think it was so durn funny if'n it was you that caught the lead. I'd be dead if it weren't that your aunt put me whole that night. Twice, in fact. Once for blood and once for water. She sure took a fuss to me."

"She sure did. Aunt Fern was one tired woman when she unhitched the mules that morning. I could see the tired and the strain on her face when she popped you into that boiling tub of mustard water, like a de-feathered fowl."

"I sure do like Fern."

"You'd better, Tit Smith. She likes you."

"And I like *her*."

"How about me?"

"I surely do like Fern Bodeen," I said, trying like crazy to hold back a giggle.

"If you didn't have that bullet hole, I'd give you an iron doughnut."

"What's an iron doughnut?"

"A good belt in the brisket. But I won't if you tell me how you got shot."

"On a Saturday night in Cornwall, Vermont. I was coming home from a dance, minding my own business; so naturally somebody just had to up and do me in. Amy, it's such a strange thing, I don't even believe it myself. Almost like it never happened. The same shot that hit me also hit Millie."

"Who's Millie?"

"Millie Sabbathday was my mother. She changed it to Millie Smith."

"Then you're real name *is* Smith."

"Tit Smith. Ain't it grand?"

"I've heard plenty worse."

"My name won't always be Tit Smith."

"You plan to change it?"

"I plan to change more than that. The change of my name will only be a sideline."

"What was your father's name?"

I was afraid that Amy was getting around to give that question an ask. And I couldn't conjure up a ghost of an answer. I just layed there on my back, looking up at the roof of the shack, with my shirt still pulled up under my chin and my white belly with its two buttons as naked as a turnip.

"Come on, Tit. You can tell me."

"Matter of fact, I'd like to tell you. I'd like to tell the whole doggone world who my pa is. Most of all, I'd like somebody to up and tell *me*. Namely him."

"Are you a—"

"Bastard? That's me, Bastard Smith."

"Please, Tit. Please don't ever feel sorry for yourself. I can't stand people who do. There's a lot worse things than being born with no pa."

"Like what?"

"Being born with one eye, or one ear, or one foot. Or without a good brain. Far as I can see, you're not missing a thing."

"I apologize, Amy. I was still half drunk when I stepped out of that tub. So I'll forget if you will."

"Accepted. But getting back to the other matter, Tit, you're off to a good start. You got hired on by Mr. Delano and here you are in Ironville, all ready to begin a new job with Ostrander."

"George Washington Ostrander," I said. "Now

that's what I call a real man's name. Maybe I could be George Washington Smith."

"I own up," said Amy, "that George Washington is a bit more high-toned than Tit. But stop making mirth for a minute. Or are you joking so you don't have to be serious about things? People do that, you know. They laugh at what hurts 'em the most, so that no one will know it gives 'em grief."

"You're right, Amy. They do. Millie did, and I guess I do. So does Gus."

"Who is Gus?"

"Friend of mine. You might say Gus is about the best friend I got in the whole wide world. If not the best, at least the oldest. He's the sheriff in Cornwall, but he actually does the sheriffing for the whole county. His name is August Tobin. Maybe that's a name for me. August Smith."

"There you go again."

"Go where?"

"Going where people go to hide a hurt. Inside a joke."

"When you laugh, it don't matter so much."

"Kiss me."

I kissed Amy Hallow with everything that I had in me. She rolled close to me with her face close to my face, so that she could touch me with her breasts and her legs. Loving her made me feel sweet and good. Like I couldn't ever do a mean

129

thing again to anybody, or mouth a mean word. Because doing anything that wasn't right and proper suddenly seemed to be such a waste of time. And time should be used for loving and touching and being near to someone, in so many old ways that seem so new and fresh. I felt like me and Amy coined it all.

I wanted to shuck off all my clothes, to feel the wind from under the doorcrack. She was in my arms, not saying a word, and it was like holding a bunch of flowers. Every once in a while, we'd retreat from each other to a distance of arm's length and I would look at her face. She would look at me. It was as if some good person had took hold of a big bar of soap and washed out all the bitters.

I don't know how long Amy and I lay before the fireplace on that blanket. Hours maybe. The fire went near out, and there was plenty of black spots all through the bed of red coals. My shirt was still unbuttoned but I wasn't cold, not with Amy as close as charity. I didn't think about Millie at all, or wonder who killed her and wounded me. Or who my pa was. Amy just filled up my heart so full it was about to bust with being so joysome.

Sometimes during the night we were asleep. But at other times, we'd be awake—looking at each other, afraid that our discovery would be lost; or slip away in the dark and we'd never be able to whistle it home again. Lying wakeful on a hard

130

floor was no fit preparation for my first day's work with Ostrander's crew, but I didn't care. I felt strong. If I was to cut timber, I'd just grab those trees with my hands and yank 'em up by the roots. Swallow 'em whole and spit out logs.

Amy was sleeping by my side. Her soft face was up near my shoulder, and I could hear the gentle whisper of her breath as it touched my ear, and it smelled like apples. I kissed the tip of her nose as gentle as I could, and she didn't even smile. Amy was far off asleep, and in a minute so was I.

"What in the name of the Devil's Drawers is this?" bellered out the make-no-mistake voice of Fern Bodeen. She weren't exactly in the best of spirits.

"Tit," she said not too quiet, "how come I turn my back on you two for a night, and here you be on the floor next to Amy with your shirt half off and your britches loose?"

"Well," I said, rubbing my eyes a bit and trying to set up, "Amy was looking for my bullet hole."

"And *you're* looking for trouble."

18

The scream that I heard early that morning was a long, high-pitch scream. Even though I was asleep, I knew that it was so sharp a sound that its maker could be doing just one thing. Dying.

Fern had bedded down herself and Amy in bunk beds (Fern below, Amy above) in one corner of the shack, and me in the other direction. As I was sleeping, my ear was real close to a gap in the clapboard. And it was through that crack I heard the scream. It was a cry that was full of pain, more pain than any living thing could stand. A scream that had to die.

Amy was a light sleeper and always heard everything, and she was down and out of her bunk to shake awake Fern. The doc heard it, too.

"What in hell was that?" said Fern.

But she weren't idle. The big Montgomery

132

Ward "Texas Ranger" shotgun got loaded with a firm click as she snapped the barrel into its latch. Amy and I were out of the door ahead of her, but old Fern (gun and all) weren't more than a pace behind. It wasn't morning and it wasn't night anymore. Just a soft swirly in-between December firstlight that couldn't decide between gray sky and white snow. As the scream come from back of where the mules was boxed, the three of us ran around the corner and saw the biggest damn dog I ever saw. But if that dog ever saw us, he didn't show it. He was too busy ripping at a man's throat. The man's face was badly tore and bleeding.

"Sabatis," said Fern, and fired.

The dog let out a yell and went off into the woods, part of his paw torn away. The snow under where Sabatis was lying was nothing but a lake of red sop. He was still breathing when we got to him, but that's about all. Each breath was a drawed-in wheeze that rattled in his throat. As her knees hit the snow to tend him, Fern tossed me the big shotgun—still smoking from burned powder.

I was on my knees, too; down in the snow, more curious than helpful. That redhide Indian looked up at me with black eyes that would never close again. I sure didn't have to be told that Sabatis had a grudge for me, for some reason. He fetched up a leathery hand and ripped out a handful of my curly red hair, and threw it in my face.

133

Then he died.

My mouth was open and I was breathing real hard from the shock of it all, besides my head hurting with pain and bewildering. I knew Sabatis didn't take to me personal. I knew it early yesterday morning, back in Ticonderoga, when we were all having breakfast in Fern's kitchen. I felt his hatred then. But as he threw hair into my face, which was his kind of a dirty insult, I saw it for myself. Even though my head hurt, and I was still half asleep, my brain started asking a question. What did old Sabatis know about me that I didn't even know myself?

"God," said Fern, who hardly ever took the Lord's name lightly—her being of the Baptist persuasion—"this sure has been one hell of a night of dying. Ray Cox, and now this one here. I wonder who in hell is going to be next."

When she said it, my back give a shudder. It was more than cold. I was real sick of dying. Millie. Me, almost. Ray Cox (who I didn't even know), and now an old redhide who even smelled bad in winter and who had done worse than spit in my face for a cause I didn't know.

"Fern," I said, "you and Amy go inside the shack and rest up. I'll bury Sabatis."

"There's a shovel in the shed," said Fern.

There wasn't much burying to do, as the snow was deep and the ground froze up. All I could do

134

for Sabatis was quilt him over with snow. I didn't know if they was wolves or coydogs in Ironville. The animal that killed Sabatis wasn't wild. I was almost dead sure that dog had wore a collar. Hard to tell for certain. I weren't certain of anything any more. Damn! There were questions I wanted to ask that old man. But with him I buried the answers.

It sure was a night for finding things:

First item I found was a bottle of whiskey in the folds of the blankets that Sabatis had wrapped around him. The bottle was near empty. Not being a drinking man, I buried the bottle with its former owner. The next thing I found, as I put the spade to snow, was a toe of an animal. The flesh was soft and smelled fresh-killed, so I reasoned it was the toe that Fern shot off the dog. I put the toe in my pocket, along with my third find—a ball of lead. I felt the lead and it was still warm from Fern's "Texas Ranger" scatter gun. Where it'd hit a rock or froze wood, it had flatted out like a penny on one side. The yonder side was as round as a ball of gunshot was meant to be. I put the lead in my pocket, too.

There was a pile of small rocks near where I was working, so I thought it only fit to use some. I'd a been hard put to say I held any affection for old Sabatis, dead or alive. But it just weren't Christian to let that animal come back for him. So after I

135

got Sabatis mounded, I coated the mound of red snow with a cover of rock. It weren't much of a cairn, not fancy at all. But it was only intended to be until spring, at which time he could be rested proper.

It weren't Sabatis that I should get buried proper, I was thinking as I piled on each rock with a cold hard "clink." It was Millie.

Had to get back to Cornwall and see her rested away like a real fine lady. I made a note in my mind to write a letter to Gus. I didn't like the idea of being anywhere and not having Gus Tobin know where I was. There just had to be a post office in the town of Ironville. What was it that old Sabatis named the place? Ad-iron-dack. Where iron is. My brain was sure dancing around from one thought to another. Since Millie died, I couldn't seem to stop thinking and just lie in bed at night, being me. There was too many questions and not enough answers to go around. Did old Gus Tobin have the right to have me took back to Cornwall and put away somewhere as a ward of the county? If he did, would he? Another thing, Gus knew more than he let on. He knew more than his prayers. Fern did, too. I got to wondering if Fern and Gus were at all acquainted. If they were, then Amy didn't know it. I decided no.

It was light now, and time for breakfast. Which was exactly what Fern was cooking when I got back inside the shack. I'd been working barehanded and my fingers were stinging red with cold, and wet from handling the rocks. Fern didn't say anything, but she did hand me a white mug of hot tea to put my hands around. It was too boiling hot to even sip on.

Amy had gone back to sleep over in the top bunk on the "ladies side" of the one room. One of her hands was growing out of the coverlets, and it made me want to touch it and feel it touch me. Fern saw me looking Amy's way.

"There's been enough trouble for one night, boy. Keep your mind to breakfast."

Fern shoved a plate of eggs and slice pork under my nose. She sat at the small table in the shack and looked at me over her teacup. She wasn't eating breakfast. Instead, she had a cup of tea—and a cud of her favorite taffy in her mouth and was sucking away on it.

"Stay away from Amy," she said in an even voice that was all business and made me stop eating before I even got started.

"About last night," I said. "Honest, Fern. We didn't do anything wrong."

"I know you didn't. Because I already asked my niece a question that I hated myself for asking, on account of which it really's none of my blessed business. But seeing as Amy's my charge and living under my roof (and you, too) I guess I got the

137

right to know what might need medicine when it's too late for morals."

Almost a minute went by and Fern didn't say a thing. She just chewed her candy real slow, twisting the candy wrapper in her fingers like she meant to choke it. Or me. My belly started to shake, watching Fern's hands twist the paper. It was like she was suddenly somebody else and not Fern anymore. I felt the heat back of my eyes. I wanted her so much to be Fern.

"Let me say to you now, Tit. Just because I found you on the Shoreham road, patched you up and drug you home, it sure don't mean I aim to have you for a son-in-law nephew. A wedding for Amy is years away. It ain't going to come earlier by a redheaded brat in her belly. So you stay away from her, understand?"

"I understand plenty."

"If I catch you playing up to her again, looking like you want to trespass on her, I'll more than run you off. I will gun . . . you . . . down."

Fern threw the yellow candy wrapper on the table so hard that it bounced into my plate. And that's when I pulled another yellow candy wrapper out of my pocket (the one I carried all the way from Cornwall) and laid it beside hers. Real slow and easy. Both were the same shade of pale yellow, and the two together were twin butterflies.

"You won't gun me down, Fern. And what's

more, if Amy wants me to hug her and kiss her and marry her, I will."

"Don't you sass me, boy."

"I won't sass you, Doctor Bodeen. And you won't gun me, neither. Because I ain't the only one who knows that you gunned down my mother."

19

"Tit, I'm spellstruck. I don't know what to say. Except that I'm sorry your ma got killed. But you know *I* didn't do it."

"You are going to hang, Doc. For pulling the trigger. I seen you work that big gun of yours and you make it sing out real smart. You'd train it on Sabatis for leaving us, and at me for being with Amy. You'd kill a person as easy as a coydog."

"Tit, you got the wrong notion. It wasn't me killed your ma."

"Hell you didn't. You got something against Millie. I can tell, so own up about it."

"Believe me, Tit."

"See this candy wrapper, Doc?"

"What about it?"

"You just twisted it up the way it is and throwed it at me."

"What's that prove?"

140

"Just this," I said, pointing to the second candy wrapper. "The one I just hauled out of my pocket I brung all the way from home. If you tell me you weren't in Cornwall, Vermont, two Saturday nights ago then I'm calling you a liar."

"That don't prove I killed your ma. A candy wrapper don't prove a thing."

"Maybe this will." I pulled two balls of lead out of my pocket and dropped the pair of them on the hard plank table.

"Are them what killed your ma?" said Fern.

"No," I said. "But the same gunblast that hit her put this here round one into my gut and you know where. This other one with the flat side come from the load you loosed at the dog that tore up Sabatis."

"Look at 'em again, boy."

I picked up the two balls of lead. They were both the same size and weight, and I was sure they come from the same gun. But as I looked closer, I could see that the two balls weren't poured from the same lead.

"One's black lead from Ticonderoga," said Fern, "and the other one, the one that you got the hard way, that's silver lead. A fool can see that. You still think I killed Millie?"

"You were there," I said. "Don't lie to me, Fern. Just look me in the eye and tell me the straight of it. You were there."

"I was there." Fern let out a sigh.

"You didn't kill my mother?"

"No, boy. I didn't kill your ma. And I don't believe you could ever think it was me who done it."

"But you were there, Fern. You know who cut Millie down. If you didn't do it, how come you were there?"

"It all started a long time ago, Tit. Way back before you or Amy got whelped. In a way, it begun with my sister, Emma Bodeen. She married up with a farmer north of town. His name was Hank Hallow. The good Reverend Harmon performed the ceremony and about a year passed by when Amy got born."

"What's all this to do with my mother?"

"I'm coming to that, boy. Hank used to go crosslake to Shoreham to trade horses with Vermont folks. Trotters, mostly. Emma went along sometimes, but not after she took sick. It was her lungs. So later on, Emma would stay to home when Hank went crosslake to Shoreham or to Cornwall to horse trade. And on one of those trips he met up with your ma, who used to live in Ti. When she moved away, I guess she went by the name of Smith. When you said you was Tit Smith, I didn't put a link to it. Smith is a common name."

"Keep talking," I said.

"Well, I remember when Hank courted Millie

back in Ticonderoga. Around the time that Millie got herself in trouble. You know, in a family way."

My stomach hurt. A slow pain started somewhere in my gut (near the bullet hole) and spread up into my chest. It was like a fever.

"Millie and Hank went around together as kids. Emma was younger than me; younger, smaller, and prettier. When Hank and Emma started to court, I'd wager that Hank Hallow was still wet behind the ears."

"Where does my mother fit the picture?"

"Like I say," said Fern, "it seems like Hank Hallow started going to Vermont to see more than horseflesh. Your ma knew Hank was married to Emma, but I guess it didn't matter a whit to her. Millie could of been jealous of Emma for catching and roping Hank. Anyhow, that was about the time Amy was born; and Emma took sick and Hank took to the bottle. Them two would fight all night. So I guess Hank packed up and told Emma he was going to Cornwall to settle down with Millie."

"What happened then?"

"It was winter, like now. Hank run off, and Emma followed and froze to death. They found her body down on the lake shore that looks across to Larrabee. In her arms was Amy, almost dead with cold. Amy wasn't even six years old."

"Is this the true of it, Fern?"

"There's more. When Millie found out about Emma's death, she didn't want Hank no more. And a month or two later, Hank Hallow was found dead drunk. And dead to boot. Millie had her revenge. Whether she knew about Amy is anybody's guess. My guess is yes. There was a measure of spite in your ma. Millie Sabbathday was a bitter woman."

"She had cause," I said. "And I'm it."

"Maybe so," said Fern. "But her own trouble didn't give Millie no right to break up Hank and Emma. And to orphan Amy."

"Seems you left out some explaining of yourself, Fern. Is that all the story?"

"No," said Fern. "Five years back, John Sabbathday died in Ticonderoga. He was Millie's pa. It was the Harmons who took him in, fed him and all. John was broke up inside over his daughter Millie getting in a family way and leaving town. After that happened, John didn't amount to beans."

"I don't understand all of this."

"You will," said Fern. "When her father died five years ago, Millie come to Ti to the funeral. Perhaps the Harmons knew where she was hid out, and the Reverend notified her of your grandfather's death. So that's when I saw your ma, Tit —all gussied up at the funeral. And I learned she then went back to Cornwall."

144

"And you followed?"

"Not for five years, Tit. But I wanted to face Millie and tell her off, just to even the score for Emma and Amy. I hated Millie enough to skin her with a dull knife."

"Enough to kill her?"

"I admit it, boy. I hated your mother like a crow hates an owl. But to be honest, I guess I resented my sister in the same way. Millie and Emma were both so damn comely, and I guess I was just the big horse of a gal who wasn't. Sometimes I even hold it against Amy, because she's so pretty. So to be honest, Tit, I had a bit of envy in my heart. Some of it's still there."

"I reckon it is."

"So a couple of weeks back, I had to take a trip over Vermont way. I stopped off in Cornwall to see kin and saw your ma on the street. Didn't even say howdy to her, or she to me. She looked so tired and beaten, I didn't have the heart. All I could feel was pity for Millie Sabbathday. I just stood there in my boots and watched her cross the street through the snow and go up some stairs over a restaurant."

"That was where we lived, Millie and me."

"Figured as much. That was a Saturday noon, the same day I left Cornwall and went up to Middlebury to see people I know—to get Amy into school there. I was several days in Middlebury. I also got a gentleman friend there that I hadn't seen in years. Besides, there was one hell of a snowstorm. So I gave Jack and Jenny a rest, and did some cooking on Mantrap."

"Where was Amy?"

"She didn't go. She had school to go to, so Amy stayed in Ti with the Harmons. But to get back to my story. While I stayed in Middlebury, I got thinking bitter about Millie and I still wanted to face her and tell her off good."

"So you went back to Cornwall?"

"I did. Pulled the wagon to a whoa and went up them stairs over the something-or-other restaurant."

"The Maple House."

"Wasn't anybody there. The place was dead as church on Monday."

"I know. I was staying with Gus and my mother was dead. She was killed on a Saturday night. And you went to pay call on her."

"It wasn't me, Tit. Not that night. I was there above the restaurant only on the night I found you on the road; and I was eating candy, like always. I looked around the place long enough to curse my luck, and left. Headed for Shoreham and home to Ti."

"That must of been the same night I run away," I said.

"It was slow going that night," said Fern, "and my girls couldn't make much time with wheels instead of runners. Lots of snow on that road, some packed and some not. I'll never know how you caught up to me, boy."

"Even been run by coydogs?" I said.

"Not me," said Fern. "But I seen the fright on the face of a dead man who was."

"That's how come I caught up to you that night."

"I'm glad I was there, Tit. And I'm grateful for a lot of things—like you coming to live with us, if only for a short spell. Most of all, I'm glad it wasn't me who wounded you and killed your mother."

"I'm glad too, Fern."

"I knew Millie had a kid. But if I'd a knowed he'd be a boy like you, Tit . . . well, I guess I don't have to say more. I never thought I'd feel thankful to Millie Sabbathday, but I sure am. For borning you."

I looked at Fern's face. She weren't the killer in my mind's eye like I figured she might of been. She was Fern again. She was big warm Fern with blue eyes and blonde pigtails. She was the lady with hands that could pick up a broken egg like me and put it back together again. Suddenly there was a lot of grief that I wanted to empty out and Fern's shoulder seemed the best place to do it.

Fern knew what I was thinking. Her big arms were around me about as fast as mine around her.

147

20

"Boy!"

What a sight! It sure was the biggest thing I
ever did see. Around noon the next day I was supposed to meet my new boss (early that morning),
but he didn't show face. So I just roamed up the
hill to the village green to take a look at old Ironville. I was plumb tuckered out from all the doings
of the night before—Sabatis died, I kissed Amy,
and then found out all that about my mother. My
eyes were so tired, the lids were at half mast. But
what I saw of-a-sudden-sure opened up my eyes
in a hell of a haste.

Six yoke of oxen (and that's a dozen of them
big beasts) in a double line, hauling a log to the
village square; a log that made a railroad car look
puny. The oxen was coming through snow that

was almost knee deep, but it didn't slow them down a whit. Not a dozen of them brutes.

Riding that log was a man in a wide-brim hat and a bright yellow mac. He just stood up high on the front butt of that log, making his long willow wand snake thru the air. Twelve oxen and each a ton weight, and every ox branded on the flank with a *GW* inside a big *O*. And up top, there was one man with nothing but a long whippy wand to guide thirty thousand pounds of beef. The oxen were Holsteins, and every ox was mapped out so black-and-white careful, like each one had been painted by an artist. And one man worked 'em all. The man in the yellow mac who stood on the front end of that log, the toes of his boots almost hanging over the top of that giant circle, and his wand swinging out a long, lazy whistle as it cut the cold.

"Now you know," said Fern, who appeared suddenly from behind me as I backed out the road, "now you know why he's the boss. Ain't another logjack in the whole north-country wilderness that could work six yoke of oxen, and make 'em chorus."

"Is that—"

"That's him. George Washington Ostrander."

"Yow."

"He does it every year."

"Does what?"

"Brings a Christmas log to Ironville. That there log was cut a year back so it'll season."

"Where's he take it to?"

"You'll see."

Fern and I followed to the rear, behind the butt end of the log, as it got drug through the snow like a big brown moon. So did half the folks in town —kids, dogs, and grown folks—all cheering the log and the man who rode it. Ostrander wasn't smiling, and he didn't look to be too friendly a cuss; but he was shouting to just about every soul who turned out. And yelling down a warning to the men below who was throwing roller logs behind the drag yoke, to give the giant log something to roll forward on.

It was peaceful to see. He turned the lead yoke without touching 'em even once with that switch. The village square turned out to be a triangle, and that's where the oxen finally stopped. About fifty or sixty paces in front of the Moravian church. Each ox halted at a given bark, and took not one step more. Their breath poured out like white feathers that curled around as if they didn't know where to go before melting away into the cold air—like a song that somebody quit singing.

"Hey, Doc!"

Ostrander yelled to Fern as he sat down on the giant log, then leaped into the soft snow, not more than a spit away. He wasn't a very big man. Standing to the front of me, I doubted that Ostrander was even three inches taller than I was. Maybe not even that.

"This here," said Fern, "is your new hand."

"Who says?"

"Mr. Delano, that's who."

"He sign you on in Ti, boy?"

"Yes, sir."

"Sir? That ain't necessary. Not here in the outback of Ironville. What's your name, boy?"

"Smith," I said.

"Where you from?"

"Vermont."

"Good state, Vermont."

"Yeah."

"You had yourself a noontime yet?"

"No. Reckon I could eat some."

"Then come on with me, boy. We'll go up to the cook shack and see what's in the pot that ain't nine days old. When your friend Fern ain't here, we don't eat so good."

"That reminds me," said Fern. "Tomorrow is Christmas. So if you bunch of mangy woodhooks want any sort of Christmas dinner, I better start stuffing hens and baking hams."

"You better, Fern. Me and my boys think of you a cook second and a mill doctor third."

By the way Ostrander squeezed out a wink in

Fern's direction, I figured I won't ask what come first.

Fern turned away to mumble some words to Mr. Ostrander, so I tried to look with interest at the oxen. The one closest to me was the left ox of the drag yoke—a big black-and-white brute with soft brown eyes. It sure was an amazement how a ox could look so gentle and be so strong. I touched him to feel if he was still warm from pulling. He was, as warm as Mantrap.

"You coming, Smith?"

"Yes, Mr. Ostrander."

"Call me G.W. Or just plain Gee, like you say to an ox."

We headed for the cook shack, and it was all I could do to keep up. My new boss sure stepped out smartly. I noticed before that he weren't a big man, nor did he move like one. His step was light, even in boots—and for a logger his walk was near to graceful.

We ate in the cook shack, on tin plates that were piled up high with yellow squares of cornbread (which my boss called Johnny Cake), pieces of steaming mutton, a Spy apple, and a heap of pink beans that sort of tumbled on each other as the mound flatted out. Ostrander ate two meals to my one. Next to Sam Callum, the blacksmith I knew back in Shoreham, I don't guess you could meet a man to out-eat Ostrander. He really could pile a plate. Seemed to burn it up just hefting his fork back and fro. We both dug in real heavy, and almost made work of it. We both saved a corner of bread to mop the bean gravy off our plates.

"Come with me, Master Smith, and I'll show you something."

"What?" I said, as we got up and went outside to a large fenced-in pen behind the cook shack.

"A dog."

It sure was a dog. One hell of a doggone big dog; and when I stepped into his pen alongside of Ostrander, I had a hunch I'd seen that dog before. Less than a day ago, and right after I buried the man that maybe this dog took apart. I looked real careful to make sure. His paw was missing toes and the wound was fresh. So fresh that the hardpack snow in his pen had brown spots. I was dead sure this was the animal that killed Sabatis. My hand felt inside my pocket for a dog's toe. It was there.

"His name is Turk. Keep your distance, dog."

The dog didn't come. And I could see why, because George Washington Ostrander was about the last thing that dog cared for. Except for one other thing, about which I was soon to get learned on. The dog just stood in its pen, growling at Ostrander; and it didn't even bother to look my way—like I wasn't even there.

"Boy," the boss said to me, "I hear from your friend, the good doctor Fern Bodeen, that some wild animal up and kilt an Indian around here last night that you put under snow."

"Yes, sir."

"Was I you, I wouldn't think no more about that there Indian. Because we don't take too kindly to 'em here in Ironville."

On a rack outside the pen, some long pieces of dried hide were hanging. It looked like hide at first, but then I knew it wasn't. Ostrander reached for one and cracked it in the air like a whip.

"This here," he said, "is the guts of a redhide Indian. And now, boy, I'm going to show you just one reason why two redhides don't breathe anymore."

Before you could even follow with your eye, he cracked the measure of dried gut so hard it pretty near cut the dog's face. The dog didn't flinch a whisker, like he expected it. He didn't charge Ostrander, but he didn't back up either. Turk just stood his ground, waiting for the next crack of gut across his face. He looked like he was too full of hate to even growl. Not once did he take his eyes off Ostrander.

"Ever since Turk was a pup, I done this to him. Every day and every night. The gut of a dead Indian's got a stink to it, or so they say. And he'll kill, he hates it so."

"You must hate that dog of yours, too," I said.

"Not me," he said. "I just hate redhides."

21

George Washington Ostrander and I spent a part of the afternoon together. Just us two.

We walked around Ironville and kicked the snow. Ostrander said he had some work to do but he didn't feel like doing it. We saw some men rolling pulpwood up two incline planks onto a wagon bed. The logs were big. Yet only two men worked a log up the ramp by using cant hooks, which was a five-foot handle on an iron jaw. When the jaws took a purchase on the log, the man would push the handle end like a lever; and hold it firm so when the other man took his turn, the log rolled up an inch or two.

We were standing near the pen where the oxen were kept. Each of us rested a foot on a fence rail and stroked the curly face of a Holstein ox. The ox poked his nose through the bars almost up to my face, in a real friendly way. But his massive size made me pull back a bit.

"He won't hurt," said Ostrander. "Not old Amos."

"Is that his name? Amos?"

"That's Amos."

"Did you name him?"

"I give every ox I own a name. Didn't use to, before I got wed to Mary. It was her doing. Mary said that each ox ought to have a name, like a dog or a cat. So each one has. All my oxen have names right out of the Bible."

"What's that one over there, the big black one?"

"Oh, that's Cain. I yoke him with the white that's rubbing his neck on the trunk of that beech tree. His name's Abel."

"How about the one with the curly horn?"

"That's Eve."

"Eve?"

"He gets a lady's name. Has to, on account he gets yoked up with Adam, the one just the other side of him."

"You named 'em all?"

"Named 'em, raised 'em, and cut 'em."

"Cut 'em?"

"Sure, boy. An ox don't get born an ox."

"I know. First it's a bull calf. Then you got to cut him to make him grow up to be an ox."

"Right. But I don't do it like some men do. I

156

seen some men cut a bull calf with a knife and let him walk away bleeding and bellering. I can't abide that."

"What do you use?"

"Telegraph wire."

"Honest?"

"The way I do it there's no pain and no bleeding. If you cut 'em, there is. So I just wind a dozen turns of telegraph wire real tight, right around the neck of the sack. Cuts off all the blood flow. And in a few days, the balls will wither and fall off dead."

"It really works?"

"It works. You're lookin' at oxen that got cut like that, every one of 'em. If you care about your stock, it's the only way to forgive the suffering."

"Sounds right to me."

"My trouble is I can't forgive. But if a man or an animal does his duty, I'm for him.

I was about to ask why he kept making Turk a killer dog by beating him with gut. But I knew why. Turk had quit his duty, and took off after a rabbit. In my mind I could see Ostrander pumping that organ with his boots and holding his little girl on his lap. George Washington Ostrander was a strange article.

Just then he reached through the fence bars and took a grip on Amos's neck. Not hard. No man could have held Amos from tossing his horns. He held the ox just firm enough, like he wanted to whisper in his ear.

"Boy," he said, "look sharp at this brute's nose. There's a splinter just inside his left nostril. Find it with your eye before you touch him. Then do it sudden. Fetch your fingers in there and pull it out with one motion. Understand?"

"I'll try."

"Don't try. Do it."

Before I touched Amos near the nose, I saw the splinter. But just as I was about to take after it, Amos decided he didn't want any part of the business. As I got hold of the wood splinter, I could see some strain on Ostrander's face. Hard to believe he was hugging Amos that still, yet he was. I pulled! Out it come, a bit bloodier than when it went in.

"You sure took your sweet time about it, boy."

Ostrander let loose of Amos. He pulled out a red bandana from the pocket of his coat and mopped the sweat off his face. I could see why. It took some holding to hold Amos. It was right then that Ostrander took his hat off. I saw him do it. He reached up his hand and pulled off his hat so he could mop the wet around his ears.

His hair was as red as mine!

It was an orange-carrot-red color that I only seen on one other human in my entire life. Me. And it made me want to take my own hat off and show him my red hair. Inside my stomach it felt like a swarm of bees. He put his hat back on, but I kept looking at his face; seeing how I might grow to look when I reached his age. I wanted to rip my hat off in a real bad-wanting way. But I held off.

I felt a funny feeling. It was like getting born, and it was a sensing that I'd felt only once before—when I read the name of Millicent Sabbathday on the paper Gus Tobin had writ on. There was a ghost inside me, a ghost of something that happened a long time back, a ghost of a thing that took place between a man and a woman. Seventeen years ago.

We walked past the giant log that Ostrander and his twelve oxen had drug to a stop in front of the Moravian church. At each end, the butts was sawed off real neat and tidy, almost like the big trunk had been wrapped for Christmas Eve. The log had been well chose. It was perfect round, with not a mark or a scar, and the bark was tight. I touched it with my hand. Even though it was a frozen spike of wood, it had a warm to it. Maybe the warm weren't in the wood; maybe it was inside me. Was I the son of Millicent Sabbathday and George Washington Ostrander?

Maybe, just maybe, I weren't to be Tit Smith all my life. But now weren't the time for change. It weren't proper to announce myself to Ironville as T. S. Ostrander. Best I keep it all to myself like a fly in a bottle, and not get too het up about it. Keep my pants on, as Gus would say. More than that, keep my hat on and not let nobody see my carroty hair, except for Fern and Amy. This is what I was thinking on when Ostrander turned on me with eyes as mean as a stud horse and punched a finger at my chest.

"Mind you, boy. You ain't to repeat the things I say to you, about what's past. Let the dead stay buried. No one in this town is going to say that G.W. went soft in the head or in the heart about oxen. You hear?"

"I hear."

"Ironville is my town. I own this burg and everything in it, such as it is. I own the wood on it and the iron under it. The jacks that cut for me are an ornery bunch, so I can't afford them thinking me going soft. Some of the men I boss are twice my size with half my brains. I don't aim to lose control of what I got a rightful dominion over."

"I understand, G.W."

"Best you do, boy. What you heard this day, best you say an Amen to it and give it a leave be."

"If you're soon sorry I know about it, how come you opened up and told me? Is it because it's almost Christmas?"

"You know what, boy? I take unkindly to Christmas."

160

"How come?"

"Didn't used to. Before I got wed to Mary I'd celebrate and get drunk with a few of the wood-hooks. Sometimes I'd even go down to Crown Point or to Ti and raise a little ned. Ever seen Tim Blake's saloon?"

"I been by it. Never went in."

"You didn't miss a thing. But to tell you the true of it, Christmas ain't much with no family and it ain't nothing with no kids. I don't know why I'm taking it out on you, or on Old Man Christmas. I just am. The whole idea of Christmas turns me ugly."

"You really sour on it?"

"Sour as summer cream."

"Then how is it you and your oxen go to the bother to drag that yule log all the way to church? I hear tell you do it every year."

For a while Ostrander didn't answer my question. He just walked along, kicking a path through the snow powder. It seemed a long time before he finally cracked open all the silence and spoke up.

"The log was Mary's idea. She said if Ironville was ever going to be a town and not stay a lumber camp, townfolk bear a need to draw together. To make a circle, you got to have a center. Something to gather round."

"How did you happen to decide on a log?"

"Mary said a log was the thing to bring people

together. We're men who strain our backs to harvest timber, and wagon it. A log is our gift and a symbol of our work, Mary thought. And when it was aburn, its firelight was a symbol of our souls. That was the way she put it. Damn the Lord of Heaven. Damn the Saint Francis nation. And damn all the simple folk in Ironville who think I can keep Christmas and forget what once was. And damn you, boy, for listening."

My heart was pounding real hard and fast. There was so much I wanted to tell this man who could swear as soft as a man who was whispering in the dark to his woman. I wanted to tell him that he wasn't as alone as he believed, and that he did have a family. Not his wife and little girl, but a son. But I was afraid it wouldn't be enough. I wanted to show him Millie's picture and my red hair. But I was scared to tell him that I was *his* boy, for fear he'd say I wasn't enough. If he'd said that, I couldn't of stood there and took it. So I didn't grab the chance of telling him, and then hearing him say that all the family he ever wanted was dead and buried deep under Ironville snow.

Somehow, I think I done right not to up and tell him. I don't know why, but I had a hunch he might of already knowed I weren't just another boy that come to cut and haul Ironville spruce. In his way, maybe he was warning me not to claim the relation. He just about said that his life as a

162

husband and father was over, and now was too late to dig up frozen memories. Too late to start it all again. Sure, I could of showed him Millie's picture. But I weren't going to do it. All I am is Tit Smith, I thought to myself, and I sure as hell don't have to be an Ostrander. Or the son of one. I didn't aim to move in on a man's private grief, and tell him to his face that I'd come to take its place. Knowing Ostrander, he'd probably spit in my eye.

"Come on," he said. "We'll get you moved into the bunkhouse with the rest of the men who ain't wedded and bedded. Where's your gear?"

"Down the hill in the little place where Fern stays, and Amy."

He stopped stone still and looked at me dead quiet. For a part second, his eyes were wider than their usual slits. His face held such a hard look, it made me shake.

"Fern brung *her* along?"

"Yes."

"Well now," he said, "you just told me what I want for Christmas. I ain't had me a woman in a fist of fortnights. And I tell you true, boy. When I bunk my first night with little Miss Amy, it'll draw enough loving out of me to make do all winter. I won't be able to walk without help until the four of March. Neither will she. Because if there is one way I aim to do this Christmas, it's to

163

split that little vix into two even pieces. One in each hand."

"Like hell you will!"

That's what I wanted to say to the man. But I didn't. Inside my right boot I felt my knife twitch against my leg, like it wanted out. Just like it was hurting to cut a certain man and do to him what he'd do to a bull calf—with telegraph wire.

22

It was Christmas Eve.

From all the preparations that Amy and Fern were making, it sure was going to be the best Christmas I'd ever have. The three of us were in the little shack, and I was helping to do what took doing without much cookery.

"Tit," said Fern, who was in the act of ripping up about forty loaves of oven bread into stuffing for the roasting hens, "go fetch that big sack of salt from out the pantry and put it up on the table."

"Which one?" I said, from the pantry. "There's two bags here. Do it make a nevermind which one?"

"It sure do. Table salt's no good for salt beads. Got to have barn salt, 'cause the crystal runs bigger. Gives more glisten to the beads."

One of the bags said "table salt," so I lugged the

other bag to the table near where Amy was mixing season to add to the stuffing.

"Now," said Fern, "you ever make salt beads to decorate Christmas?"

"No," I said, "never have."

"We'll need flour and water and salt, so get a tub. Mix up the flour and water first—easy, not too much water or we'll have nought but soup—and press out little round balls of dough."

"Here," said Amy, "I'll roll your sleeves up or your good shirt'll get soiled."

"Thanks," I said.

"Spread some of that barn salt out on the table," said Fern, "and roll them little dough balls around in it, until they all-over sparkle. That's right. Amy, look in my old black valise under the bunk and get the hatpins."

"Hatpins?" I said.

"It's to make holes," said Amy. "See? We just slide this beautiful bead on the hatpin, so it'll take a set."

"You mean it'll dry up hard, like a bead?"

"Yes," said Amy. "And you have a hole right through the middle for the string to go through."

"A string of white sparkle beads," I said.

"You ain't seen nothing yet," said Fern.

"Here," said Amy, handing me three little bottles. "Now we can have four colors."

"What's that stuff?"

"This," said Amy, "is spinach juice to die some of the beads green. The red is beet juice, and the mustard begets yellow."

"Too bad," said Fern.

"Too bad about what?"

"It's a shame," said Fern, "we didn't bring enough mustard to bath Tit. He's right fond of that. Eh, Tit?"

"Look, you folks," I said. "I'm as partial to keeping Christmas as anybody. But if Christmas means another boiling in that yellow hell of yours, I rather go heathen."

"Not another mustard tub," said Fern. "But come morning, it's Christmas. You better slick up."

"I will."

"Too bad there's no barber shop in Ironville. You could do with about three haircuts."

"Yeah," I said as I stroked my chin with a salty hand, "and I suppose I could do with a shave."

"Let's see," said Fern, her cheek next to mine for a quick rub. "Maybe we ought to sop some cream on your face and let the cat lick it off. I'd hate to let them three tiny stalks of buzzard fuzz fall to a razor. Be a shame to hone an edge for them three."

"Maybe I'll grow a beard," I said.

"A great big beautiful red beard, just the color of your hair," said Amy, "and you'd look like a pirate."

"I would?"

"Yes, and when you grow old, your beard will turn snow white and you can be Saint Nick."

"Naw," said Fern. "He's too lean. With my girth and expansion, *I'd* have to be Santa. But if I was, there'd be no Christmas."

"How come?" I said.

"Because the first chimney I come down, I'd get my big fat arse stuck inside and never get out. Haw! Haw! Haw!"

Between the joke and the way Fern told it, my face was aching I was laughing so hard. Amy was laughing, too. But neither Amy or me got such a boot out of it as Fern. Before she stopped laughing long enough to wipe her eyes, there was poultry stuffing all over the floor, all over Amy, and even a crumb or two on my beadwork.

"Aunt Fern? Are we going up to see them fire the yule log?"

"Lord, yes!" said Fern. "Can't miss that or it wouldn't be Christmas Eve. Let's go. The stuffing can wait. Besides, the bread ain't stale enough. Can't make good Christmas stuffing out of fresh bread."

Uphill, on the snow-covered village green in front of the Moravian church, the big yule log that Ostrander and his twelve oxen brought was already afire. According to Fern, the men had put an auger to all sides of it to make holes. Then poured in

168

kerosene. Lit up, the giant log looked to be burning —which it was. But no log that size would of ever fired that good without plenty of starter flames.

Far as I could see, the church was the one lonesome church in town. All the folks of Ironville had turned out, or so it seemed, whether they was Moravian or no. Sure was a picture. As we came up the hill, the first thing we awared of was the music. All of Ironville was singing. It sounded like they wanted the whole black wilderness of Adirondack to know that there was one tiny light inside the sea of pines and spruce and hardwood that went away from us in all directions. One tiny light inside all the miles of blackness. Like when you're all alone in the middle of the night, and you strike a match.

Coming closer, we saw the people with their backs to us, singing to the log. Against the yellow light, they stood like an uneven row of black statues, making an offering of music to the flame.

Everyone sang.

It weren't like church, where only some did. Big men sang, with faces that you'd think would be empty of music. They sang the warm and honest Moravian hymns in voices rough as tree bark. The words told about the Baby born in Bethlehem, and their voices seemed to sweeten the story. It was about Mary, too. The women who stood at the elbows of their menfolk sang as well. Their cheeks were pink with firelight, and softened by their belief in the long-ago birth of a child on a cold and snowy evening.

Plenty of children were on hand. But not to tomfool or raise Cain. Most of the young ones stayed close to their mothers, their wide eyes drinking in the loglight. Some of the older girls and boys sang a strange melody that seemed to fly around the real tune without meeting.

Fern and Amy and I stood together in the snow. We sang together, like a family. Like the three of us was oak beam, fit to corner a barn and stand forever. Something that would really hold hay. We were *my* family. I didn't need nobody else. We stood close to each other in the cold to warm each other with nearness. In a triangle we stood: Fern to the rear, Amy and me up front and close by. Behind us, we could feel the big cozy belly and bosom that was Doctor Fern Bodeen. Only she was so much more than a doctor, or a cook. She was someone that Amy and I would always stand by and hold to. More than anyone in the whole world, I wanted to grow up to be like Fern. Big and able, gentle and laughing—that was Fern.

As we stood there singing, I forgot all else. I wasn't even Tit Smith anymore, but the new me didn't need no father or no name. It was like an old stump I seen, back in Cornwall. The stump was big and rotted out, dead as can be. But as I come

170

closer to it, a bird flew out. She flew around my head to chase me off, and I knew there was life in that stump. Down in the dark, wet rot, there was a nest with birdlets.

And that's how I felt, singing. Like there was a bird in me that I didn't know was there. It made me part of a nest. I was an old stump until the songbird in me flew out, and it just would never stop the song. It made me decide to be the man of this family that needed a man, and I would protect these two women with all the strong I could muster. Even against Ostrander.

Later, the three of us walked back down across the white snow to where we finished our work. I got the salt beads done and dyed. They got set to dry behind Mantrap. That old stove would have a busy day come morning, with all the cookery Fern had a plan to. And because of that, the woodbox needed filling up. That was my job. So I lugged in plenty of frozen stove wood, some of which looked like somebody'd split up an old apple tree just for Fern's calefaction.

Funny thing. As the wood began to thaw in the woodbox (next to Mantrap), some ants come out. Guess they was froze up inside the wood when it was out-of-doors. In about ten minutes, we had ants all over. Seeing as Fern spilled out some bread crumbs to make the dressing, that's what they went for. Amy went after them with a broom.

Fern put on her coat and said she had an errand to run. Said she'd be back in two shakes.

After that, I was getting my gear together to move up to the bunkhouse with some of the loggers. I was sorting my duds on the blanket of my bunk, when Amy picked up a sock. She poked the tip of a pink finger through a hole in the brown wool.

"I'll darn it," she said. "And you can stop by tomorrow and pick it up."

"Thanks, Amy."

I watched her hands roll my sock into a ball, which she put in her apron pocket.

"There's a button off your shirt," she said. "I'll be glad to put it right for you."

"Aw, you don't have to. I can do it."

"I know. That's why I want to."

She sat at the edge of my bed and flipped through my old Bible that I'd brung all the way from Cornwall. It'd been Millie's. Then she stood up quickly, and her arms went around my neck.

"I know who you are," she said.

"So do I."

"No, Tit, I really mean it. Aunt Fern says it pays to read your Bible, and it sure does. Didn't you ever read inside the cover of your family Bible, where births and deaths and *names* are written?"

"No."

"In that case, I have a Christmas gift for you,"

she said, "and it's something you really want. Kiss me."

As I kissed Amy, the two of us stood alone in a big candy world of sweet goodness. Then I felt her lips crawling up to my ear, and whispering:

"Merry Christmas to you, Timothy Sabbathday."

23

I could still taste Amy.

Walking up the hill to the bunkhouse, alone through the snowflakes and the silent night, my mouth carried the sweet flavor of hers. Like after you eat pie. I was hoping she could still feel my arms hug her up close.

It was late. The bunkhouse was dark inside, so I felt my way along the row of snoring men to an empty cot. At first, before my eyes melted some of the blackness, I thought the cot was occupied 'cause some jack had hung his long lisle underwear on it. The underwear suit was soaking wet. It was draped over the high footboard—to dry, I suppose. Didn't smell too clean. The underwear just hung there, arms down on one side and legs down on the other, as tired as the man who'd soaped it.

I laid down on the bunk on my back, and folded

my hands up under my neck. Here I was, and tomorrow would be Christmas. Maybe I went to sleep
for an hour or so, but it didn't seem like sleep. It
was more like rolling around.

I heard a dog bark. . . . Turk. It sounded closer
than the cook shack. He must of slipped his collar
and got himself loose and out of his pen. Good for
you, Turk.

Now I was awake, thinking on what took doing.
This much I knew: I was going to stop George
Washington Ostrander. For a second, my head
hurt—where Sabatis had pulled out a fistful of my
red hair and flung it in my face. He knew. That
old redhide knew that Ostrander had sired me. He
looked at my face that first morning and he saw
the Ostrander look, and the Ostrander red hair.
And he hated. But he didn't hate Ostrander enough
to stand up to *him*. So old Sabatis looked at me like
I weren't worth a squat.

Well, I didn't cotton to Sabatis much either. But
I wouldn't sic a dog on a man just because he's an
Indian. What Tahawus did weren't the fault of
Sabatis. Somebody ought to even the score for that
old man, and that was *one* reason Ostrander ought
to die. Two dead Saint Francis Indians was enough
to balance out for Mary Ostrander and Nell.

Two was Turk. A beautiful dog whipped with
Indian gut to be a killer. Why in hell would Indian
gut smell any different from a white man's? To a

175

man's nose, maybe no difference. To a nose like Turk's, maybe. Like the paunch of a squirrel smells sweet of hickory nuts and apples, and the paunch of a fox is the hard-gut game smell of bone, flesh, and fur. I seen Sabatis eat. He ate dried corn and sour meat instead of hot bisquits and sow pork. And somehow Turk knew. And I swore that Ostrander would not give Turk any more beatings. Maybe I'd steal Turk for myself; or better yet, offer to buy him—and train him back to be a gentle worthless dog like he maybe once was.

So what if this redheaded log boss *is* my father, my dad, my old man? He got Millie Sabbathday in a family way and didn't marry her. Maybe run out on her, and Millie with a belly full of red-haired baby. I was glad she named me Timothy. Millie weren't all wrong. Millie made three.

Reason four was the fact that Ostrander wanted to bed up with Amy. Not take her to wife. Just take her. Put another redhead boy in her belly, like he done to Millie. I swore he'd never touch Amy Hallow, and I would wind telegraph wire around him before he did.

I had to admit that reason number five was the most important. And it come down to Ostrander or me. Ostrander and son. When he finds out I love Amy—and worse, that she sort of cottons to me—if'n he would tear up a Indian for spite, he'd get *me*. I had me a feeling, were George Washington Ostrander to catch me sparking Amy Hallow, he'd rip me belly to brisket. I'd be dead before I hit ground. Gus Tobin said there was only one morality and that was survival.

I will stop this man, even though he is my own father. Because somebody sure as hell got to make the man quit, and I don't guess that leaves a soul besides me. Worse than my vow to do it was this: I'd set a trap for Ostrander, and bait the trap with Amy. You catch a coon thataway. And a possum. I really hadn't even killed much of anything before, except a big rat under Millie's bed. Can't say I pleasured it much. Helped old Gus Tobin kill a chicken one time. Cut her throat. To cut Ostrander's gullet, I'd have to face him. And I knew it was going to be like murdering half of me. The Ostrander half.

I sure wish I was home in Cornwall. Back home where August Tobin was the law. There weren't no law in Ironville except for one kind: Ostrander law. Everywhere you looked in this town there was a cussed big *O* with a *GW* inside it. Every ox wore it. It was even burned on the butt end of the big yule log. I swore one thing. There wouldn't be no *GWO* on Amy. And no *GWO* on me. He didn't itch to be my pa seventeen years ago. I weren't about to be his son. No sir, daddy mine. Not this boy.

In the dark, lying on that cot, I smiled. The laugh was on Ostrander, who did not know I was

177

his son. I'd been careful about that. Never even took a leak without my hat on. That was my edge. He didn't know; I did. Would he ever suspect? We'd ate noonmeal together and he faced me, yet he didn't guess. And he looked right at my Ostrander face.

He was my father. And in a way, I felt pity for a lonely and bitter man. There was a sorry sickness in him that no love could ever heal. Not even mine. He was a stranger and an enemy, and I felt nothing toward him—except for a want-to-get-even feeling that burned in my belly as cold as winter iron. It sure didn't help to think that I might murder somebody. It was wrong and all wrong. But what else was there? What law was there for the Ostranders of the world, the people who hurt other people and hurt 'em so bad that it spread like a fever? Millie's hurt that spread to Amy's pa and ma and left her an orphan for Fern to raise. Maybe even back to Ostrander.

And my hurt. Millie's hurt got long-ago choked to death in a bottle and in a bed. But not mine. It was the day I went fishing with Will Barnum back home in Cornwall. The fish weren't biting. So we just sat in the shade and swapped lies. He'd tell and I'd tell. Then after, when we run out of false, we sort of started on the truth.

Will was talking about the fishpole he had in his hand, and how his pa made it for him. He said how good his pa was at making things—like fish rods and baseball bats and saddles. Will's old man even made him a skinning knife, and bored out the handle out of a real antler. Will went on and on about how his pa taught him to whittle, and hack a whistle out of spring poplar. I guess what hurt me most is the fact that Will was my friend, and yet he didn't hold an inkling on how it felt to me, all the things he told me about *his* pa. I just wondered how he could of gone on talking about fathers.

Didn't he know? Weren't a soul in Cornwall who didn't know a truth or two about Millie and her bastard kid. They even called me "Millie's boy," like I had no name. It was like they knew that the Smith part of it was just a lie, which it was. The name of Millie Smith had no truth to it, and neither did Tit Smith. It weren't an honest name, and it seemed to fit proper for a boy who wasn't even a person.

Two things I wanted to do, I thought as I lay on my cot: bury the name of George Washington Ostrander in the ground; and bury along with it the name of Tit Smith. And it'd be right welcome to do a third thing: change Amy's name someday to Mrs. Timothy Sabbathday.

All that I'd wanted just a week ago now seemed to be small. Who killed Millie? Who was my pa? Who is Tit Smith?

Now I found some of the answers to them questions, they didn't much matter no more. Look what I found instead: I found Fern Bodeen and Amy Hallow and Tim Sabbathday. Better yet, they found me. I was now a piece of something bigger than just me. Like me and Amy and Fern and the mules and Mantrap . . . on our way up here to Ironville with smelly old Sabatis in the lead, we were a joke on wheels.

What were we? A toothless old Indian who'd never put soap to his red hide. A big belly-laughing and boot-kicking woman doctor who could have healed a whole world with either medicine or love. A beautiful sweet orphan girl who would someday be a better doctor than Fern. And by damn I'd work day and night to pay her way at Middlebury College. And their pet bastard boy that they found and fed. Along with "one smart hinny" named Jack and a mule named Jenny.

We ain't no family, I thought. We're a traveling show. A sideshow of freaks, like the one I'd see along with a circus that'd come Cornwall way. And I was the big freak of the lot. Because I had to stop a man I could of loved, but instead was a man I hated, who happened to be my pa. I had to do it in order to even the score for lots of people, and to protect the girl I wanted to be my wife someday. Hadn't asked her yet, but I would when I had enough to offer besides myself.

Planning what I was planning, it was no use to

stay on here in Ironville. I'd go back to Ti with Fern and Amy (providing I was still alive), and I'd ask Mr. Delano for a job in the Ticonderoga Pulp & Paper Company. Then I could live with Fern and Amy, and we could all save up for Amy's doctoring school. I had it all worked out.

"Hey!"

My body froze to stiff, like somebody'd kicked it that way. I heard a man's voice on the other side of the wall near my bed, coming from the outdoors.

"Come on, Fern. Don't be so doggone prissy. It ain't like you, honey."

"Got to get home, Luke." Fern's voice sounded like maybe she'd throwed back a drink or two.

"One kiss more ain't like to change things. Hell, it's Christmas Eve. The boss said I could keep you out good an' late. He said he had a reason."

Without a sound, I yanked on my boots—making sure my knife was riding where it rode, stuck in my boot-top outside my right leg. If Fern was up here, it meant one thing. Ostrander had got to Amy.

I was running again. But this time I ran like a man and not like a boy that run away from home, or like a boy that was such a fool to think he'd outrun coydogs. This time I ran smack toward the trouble. It was downhill; and as I ran, the cold air thrust deep in my chest like it wanted me stabbed.

There was boot tracks of a man that led right through the snow to the shack; and worse, the tracks were not cut fresh.

The door was shut tight, but it didn't stop me. Because I was running full tilt when I hit my shoulder to it. The boards split with a loud crack and I was on the floor among the splinters, laying there in the dark with my head about a yard away from old Mantrap. By the time I got to my feet, the knife was out of my boot and in my hand. About the same second I heard Amy crying, a hard thing hit my belly full force. It had to be Ostrander's head, and it knocked me ribs-first backward against the hot stove. My left hand got burned, but there was no pain to it; as if there weren't time for the burn to sink in. He hit me in the eye with a fist that felt like lead.

"You young bastard," he said.

"Yeah," I said, "but I ain't *your* bastard."

I made an upswing with my knife, but missed. His boot come up and got me in the crotch, and it hurt so I didn't know which hand had a purchase on the knife handle—or even if I had a knife.

His fist caught my face again, and my cheek made a squishy sound. It made me drop my knife. I tried to raise up my hands but they wouldn't lift. I wanted to duck or run or something so it wouldn't hurt anymore. His next punch would finish me and I knew I didn't hold a prayer.

As I moved my foot, my boot slipped on my knife (I guess) that was on the floor. My body fell and all of Ostrander's force went over me. The punch he was throwing at me missed, and his head must of hit the stove. For a moment he looked dead as a stump. But then he moved.

Amy's nightclothes were most tore off her and she seemed almost white naked. She was crying hard. As my hand found her shoulder, all I felt was the terrible tremble of her body. Under her on the quilt was the big 12-gauge Montgomery & Ward shotgun. Behind me I heard Ostrander coming our way. But before I could get the gun up and around, he took a hold on it too.

We fought, but he had me all the way. He pushed the gun barrel hard into my neck so I couldn't breathe. Running down the hill had spent most of my air and there weren't much left in me to choke on. Back through what was left of the broken door Ostrander pushed me, his knee coming up into my gut three or four times to make my hands let loose the gun. But I wouldn't. I could see moonlight on his face and he was nothing but hatred, for everything and everyone.

Outside now, on my back in the snow, Ostrander was on me—and I knew it was over. Choked, kicked, or beaten to death—it no longer mattered which. I wanted to yell to Amy and tell her to run. Looking up, the snow had stopped. The winter sky over Ironville had stars. So many it looked like salt on blue velvet. But all the stars were going dim, going out.

Turk hit Ostrander's neck so hard, the man was knocked plumb off me into the snow. His neck was a faucet of blood. Before I could get up, the dog had done what he had wanted to do—and there was little left of Ostrander that even the strong men of Ironville could look at without turning away their heads.

My father, George Washington Ostrander, was buried under snow . . . not twenty feet away from Sabatis.

24

7 April 1899
~~Tyconderoga~~
Ticonderoga

Dear Gus

Probly you ben wanting to know where
I run off to when I hed for Ti and also what
hapend to me. Nothing much. Accept that I
found two women to live with that I love a
hole lot and who love me. There names are
Fern Bodeen and her nice Amy Hallow Fern
is a Ti Pulp docter and a good cook. Amy
goes to school with me. I was game to quit
school but Fern said no and that gramer is
good to marry a docter with. Speling is good to.

Now that my ribs are mendid and we found

185

out that my neck weren't really broke. I do
lots of odd jobbs in town to earn money for
my keep. I will earn more when I go to
work for Ti Pulp. I saved up to buy a marble
headstone for my mothers grave. Please tell
Lucas Mix that soon I am coming Cornwall
way with a waggon to colect Millie and bring
her to Ti to bury her next to her own pa John
Sabbathday. He is my grandfather. I will
stop you can bet and say hi to you and say
thanks agian for puling out the led
     I sure do mis you Gus.
               Your friend —
           Timothy Sabbathday

P.S. I seen Ironville.

About a week or two went by after I wrote that
letter to Gus. One evening, Amy and I were
stretched out on the floor (home in Ti) looking at
a doctoring book on pathology. Fern kept looking
at us to make sure that our interest was, as she always said, "pure medical."

The doorbell rang.

"I'll go see," said Fern, "seeing as I need the motion more'n you two scarecrows."

As Fern opened the door, we didn't look up to see who it was. Mrs. Harmon, the minister's wife, often come over on account she lived nearby and liked to neighbor with Fern. Then I heard a voice.

"Tim," said Fern, "you got a visitor."

Getting up off the floor, I went to the door. There he be, standing on the front porch with his hat in his hand and a big grin on his face.

"Gus!"

He held out his right hand to shake, and then he brought up the other real slow. As if to say a handshake weren't enough. Well, maybe enough for some folks, but not for me and Gus Tobin. I give one big leap and most knocked the sheriff off Fern's stoop. It was one heck of a bear hug, and it was tough to say who hugged harder. Before he let go, he mussed up all my red hair—like he always done since I can remember. And he smelled the same, too. Like coffee and oats.

"Fern," I said, after I cut loose from the purchase we took to each other, "Fern, this here is Gus."

"August Tobin, ma'am. Pleased to make your acquaintance."

"Likewise," said Fern, "likewise. You're a stranger to the eyes but not to the ears."

"Amy!" I yelled. "Come see who's here. Amy,

this here is Sheriff August Tobin of Cornwall, Vermont. Gus, this is Amy Hallow and Fern Bodeen."

"Miss Amy, Miss Bodeen . . . I sure am beholding for all you done for Tit."

"*Tim*," said Amy, "speaks a lot about you, Mr. Tobin."

"Tim," said Gus. "Now that's a fine name for a boy who growed up as much as you."

"What we all standing here on the porch for?" said Fern. "We got a kitchen table with pie on it."

"Pie?" said Gus.

"Rhubarb," said Fern. "Fresh baked."

"Miss Bodeen, I don't recollect downing a slab of rhubarb pie since Garfield got shot."

"One order of pie coming up," said Fern, poking a finger in my ribs, "and I don't s'pect *you'd* eat any."

"Yes, please," I said.

One thing about Amy, you never need tell her a thing. She just knew. While Fern was showing Gus around the parlor, Amy gave me a pinch that meant to come and help her in the kitchen. She dished out pie and I dumped some coffee in the pot and soon it was dancing on Mantrap's front-left, like it was happy as me.

Gus was one of them wiry folks who could eat anything, and wound up by eating everything. We all sat around the kitchen table and watched him put away two wedges of Fern's pie, a moon of cheese, a brace of doughnuts; and to wash it down, three cups of coffee. We had a few Devil's Cheek apples left over in the winter barrel, and Gus made one of 'em go away.

"I love to feed a man who eats," said Fern.

"Tim," said Gus, "here's an idea. You go back to Cornwall and be the sheriff of Addison County, and I'll stay here and feed my face at Miss Bodeen and Miss Amy's fine table."

"When you planning to go back home, Gus?" I said.

"I ain't."

"You going to quit sheriffing?"

"Already quit."

"Who's going to sheriff in Cornwall?"

"Don't know. But there's a right good chance it won't be me."

"How come, Gus?"

"Well, I been the law over crosslake for twenty years. More'n that. I wanted to see what was west of Larrabee and north of Ti. Ever heard a man named Cyrus Porter?"

"Sure have," said Fern. "Owns a farm just north of town, and a fine string of trotting horses."

"He don't own 'em all now," said Gus. "We been writing letters back and forth for a couple of years. We met one September at Rutland Fair. So about a week ago, he put in at Cornwall and stayed the night."

189

"Then what?" I said.

"Cyrus is getting on," said Gus. "He's got no family, not a chick or a child. And all he's got now is a partner."

"You?" said Fern.

"Me."

"Gus, I don't believe it," I said. "You going to settle down in Ticonderoga. You always did have a way with horses. It's what you should of done years ago. How come you waited so long?"

"Reasons," said Gus.

"Like what?"

"Like my home was in Cornwall, and my job. Not to mention folks that I was right fond of, that ain't there no more."

As Gus spoke he looked my way, and I knew he meant me and Millie. I just knew he did, but couldn't bring himself up to say more. It weren't his way. Not old Gus.

"My wagon's at the livery stable next to the tannery," he said.

"Putnam's."

"Yeah, that's the place. I travel light; and besides, I don't own much worldly goods."

"You come for keeps, Gus? For honest and keeps?"

"Sure did. Hired out a team and wagon just to lug my stuff crosslake on the Larrabee barge."

"Sounds like you brung more than just a change of drawers, Gus."

"I did, Tim. I brung your ma."

"All the way from Cornwall?"

"Every turn of the wheel. Weren't no trouble, seeing as I was coming this way anyhow. So come morning, we can give Millie a right proper grounding. Like you said, Tim. She belongs to be rested in Ti earth, alongside her pa."

"Amen," said Fern.

"Thanks, Gus."

"I built the box for her myself," he said. "It ain't fancy, but it'll rest her away real fit. It's painted black and still wet."

"Gus, I sure am grateful."

"That ain't all, Tim. We got the man who put the gun to your mother."

"Who was it, Gus?"

"Nobody," said Gus. "Just a worthless drunk drifter who didn't have no job and never would. Seems like after he shot Millie he had too big a mouth."

"What was his name?"

"Not even worth remembering," said Gus.

"Where's he now? In jail?"

"I hanged him."

"You hanged him, Gus? Honest?"

"Oh, he had a trial. Even had a lawyer to defend

his side of the issue. But when I caught up with him, he still had his scatter gun and some loads of silver lead. I fired it off in the courtroom and showed the jury the lead—along beside the lead Lucas Mix took out of your ma's remains. It was like twins. The man confessed to it and cried like a wet baby. But we roped his neck to make sure he won't shoot up no one else. He won't. He's asleep in the deep, six foot closer to Hell."

"Why'd he do it, Gus—kill Millie?"

"Don't matter, boy. It's over and done with, and what's past is past. Look between the horse heads and not back yonder at wagon tracks."

"I don't know what to say. I owe you, Gus. I'm beholding."

"You sure are," said Gus. "And don't think it's a debt to be writ off. You know that horse farm north of here that I aim to own?"

"Yes?"

"Well, old Cyrus Porter won't live forever, so we'll need help. How about throwing in with us? I won't live forever neither."

"Me? You want *me*, Gus?"

"Sure do. You remember Sam Callum, the guy who shod horses and moved to Shoreham?"

"Course I remember Sam. Next to you, Sam's best."

"Sam told me you had a good way with horses. You ain't full of noise or meanness like some young bucks. Sam says you do right good with horses, the way you pare a hoof and set a shoe."

"Yeah, but—"

"I'm askin', Tim. I talked it out with Cyrus and he says to bring you along. We want some greenery around the place, on account of which I'm old and Cyrus is older."

"Nonsense," said Fern.

"You mean you don't want me to go?" I said to Fern.

"Course I do. Best thing in the world ever happened to a boy like you. I sure don't want to see you rot away in a paper mill all your life, losing your fingers one by one. What I think is nonsense is to hear Mr. Tobin say he's old. Now that's nonsense."

"Any man who leaves Vermont," said Amy, "to come crosslake and be part of a new way of living . . . is *young*."

"You're right, Miss Amy. With a gut full of rhubarb pie and a meadow full of trotting horses, Ti sure has me feeling welcome."

"Friends," said Fern. "They count for most. And to start off with, you got Cyrus Porter, and young Timothy Sabbathday, along besides Amy and me."

"Miss Bodeen, I feel like I been here in Ti all my livelong life."

"And I'll be the first one to run you out," said

Fern, "unless you quit calling me Miss Bodeen. To every soul in town, I'm just plain Fern."

"Fern it is," said Gus. "But to beg your pardon, ma'am . . . a lady with your good looks can't be called plain."

"Amy! Tim! You two going to sit around here all evening? Don't you have some lessons to study? When I your age I had chores to keep me busy. So go find some chores," said Fern, "or I'll find 'em for you."

Amy and I left the kitchen and took a walk up a hill that overlooked our town. It was April in the north country, still dark in the evening, and still cold. But the ground under our boots was awake and working. And against the sky, tree buds were aborning. We stood close to each other, laughing at how Fern had kept us apart in the past weeks. Watched us like a bulldog, until tonight.

"I know how it feels," I said, looking down from Mount Hope at the lights of Ti.

"How what feels?" Her arms were around my waist.

"How it feels to be rich."

"Me, too. Living with Aunt Fern is like living in a pantry that holds all the spice of the world."

"And all the rhubarb pie."

"I like your friend, Tim. I even like his voice, the way it runs so clear. Like spring water."

"You like Gus?"

"He's clean and straight. He's like you. When you get to know him he seems so much taller than he is. Hey, why are you shaking?"

"Because I found so much, Amy. I found you and Fern, and now Gus is here so maybe I'll find a future with horses. I didn't find who shot my mother, and I didn't find a father to settle with. But what I was looking to hitch myself to is right inside me, so I found the only man that matters."

"So did I," said Amy.

Behind us, a whipporwill sang out his name over and over, again and again. The sky was far away and cold, but Amy was nearby and warm. The land was alive and ready for the sweet work of spring.

The hard of winter was over. Deep in the earth, the April corn was almost green.

ROBERT NEWTON PECK was raised in Ver-
mont, the setting for his highly-acclaimed *A Day No
Pigs Would Die*, as well as *Millie's Boy*. *Path of
Hunters*, his recently-published story of animal strug-
gle in a meadow, is based on the author's childhood
memories and first-hand observations of nature.

Robert Peck now lives in Connecticut with his
family.